RUNE STONE
BOOK 1

THE SONS OF WODEN

Rune Stone
Book 1

The Sons of Woden

Wayne Oxley

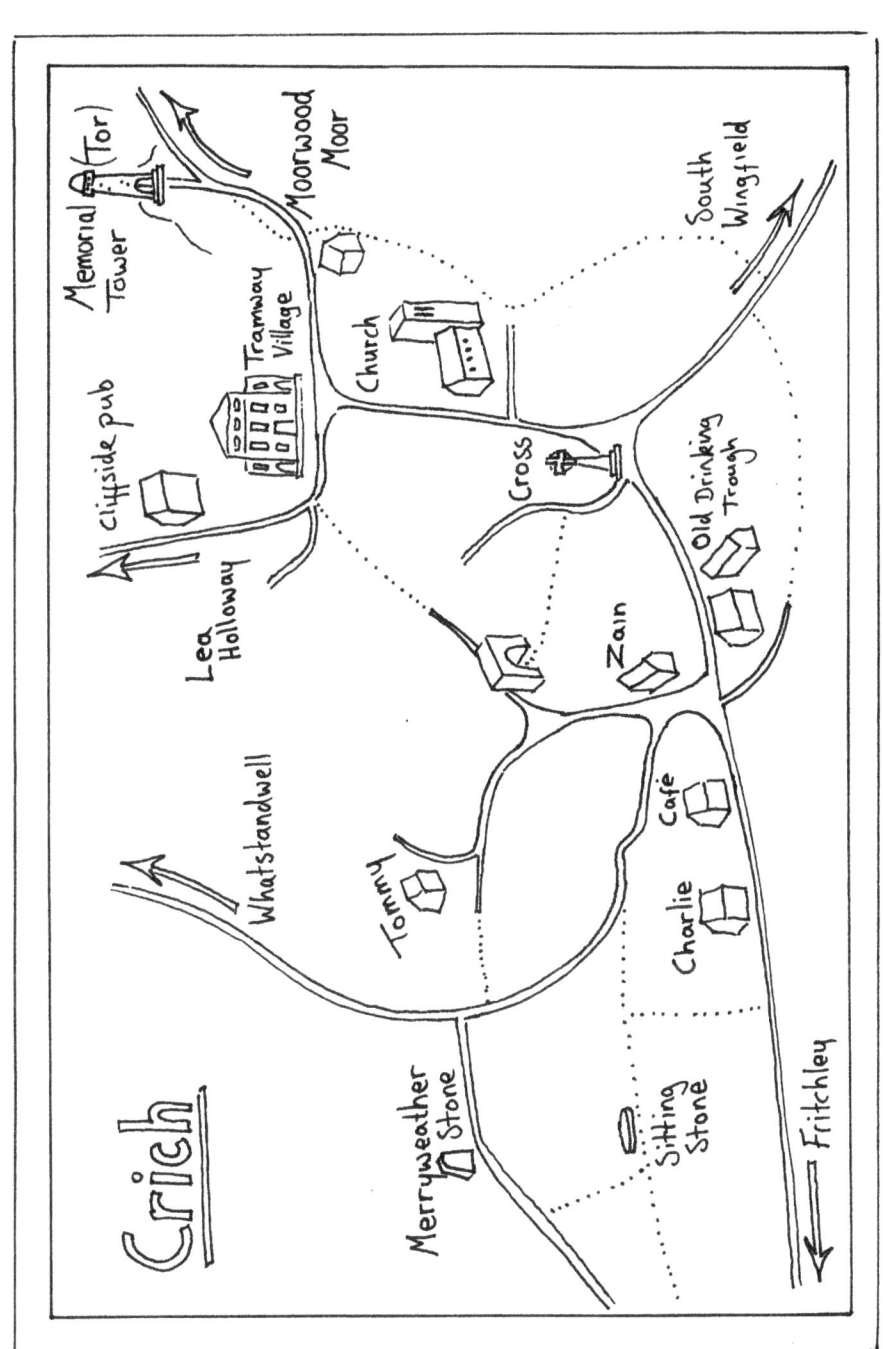

Chapter One

Across the Fields (Friday)

For as long as people could recall, the moorland had held man, woman and all of their advances at bay. Wonderous in their rugged beauty, wild and unforgiving, they remained steadfast against time itself, patiently awaiting the unwise and the foolish who dared to explore. The windswept hills, dotted with tufts of long marsh grass and sharp gorse bushes with their small yellow flowers, now brought the only relief from the dull greens and greys of the landscape as winter quickly approached. The moors were still only inhabited by a few, the odd village and farm that had managed to cling on.

Being only a short distance from their homes, Charlie and his friend Zain had made the decision to venture into this wilderness for they knew of a safe place away from the village, a place away from their troubles, a place where they alone could rule the night. They approached the 'Sitting Stone' with great anticipation for they had been promised that the outcome of tonight would be different.

Charlie and Zain were confident in their movements having made this journey numerous times, yet still they were alert, for their journey this evening had been made more dangerous by the number of cows that were taking an interest in the visitors to 'their' field. They were also wary of the number of cowpats that seemed to have been placed with strategic precision down the path.

Zain skipped on ahead through the minefield of pats in front of him artfully dodging each one while Charlie continued to contend with what now seemed like the whole herd of cows. "Come on, out of the way, this is getting tiresome now. Go and eat some grass or something." He knew that they thought he was the farmer come to take them in for the night, but it was starting to bother him just the same.

The Sitting Stone had been named that by the gang. It was only small but perfectly formed, light grey in colour, smooth on all sides and was as its name suggested, great for sitting on. Nestled neatly at the edge of the field along the path it provided fantastic views down the Derwent Valley all the way across to the Memorial Tower which stood silhouetted against the fading evening sky.

Not far now, thought Charlie.

He was looking forward to seeing Tommy who he knew would cheer him up. After the row he had just had with his mum he needed some time with his friends, away from the house to take his mind off it.

The sun was starting to set behind the hills and the sky had turned a beautiful orange. Charlie could see the first stars start to shine through and he could feel the chill air on his face, autumn was definitely here.

Should have brought some gloves, was the thought that kept running through his mind.

As they reached the final stile, they could make out the shape of Tommy. His appearance was pretty distinctive, being tall and lanky with a slight hunch from his neck. They could just make out the red stripe on the sleeve of his jacket as it reflected the last of the evening sunlight. He had worn his black hoodie most days since his birthday last month; Tommy did this quite a lot when he had a new top, t-shirt, coat or anything like that; he would just wear it to death. Now was the time for his black and red hoodie.

"You're late!" called Tommy with slight sarcasm as he caught sight of his friends.

"Yeah, well it's been difficult to get out tonight of all nights. You know how important it is to my mum to take part in the procession! Anyway, five minutes is hardly late," replied Charlie.

"It's lame."

"That's your opinion, Tommy and my mum likes the procession. Anyway, she gave in and came around to my way of thinking eventually, she was clearly not impressed though. I'm going to have to make it up at some point, so you owe me. Anyway, we're here now."

"Not the procession, your timekeeping."

"At least I can tell the time, Tommy. Hey look, don't start." Charlie was clearly tense and agitated so Tommy lay off.

"What's the plan?" Charlie carried on.

"Thought we could chill out up here for a bit then go over to the park and see if anybody else is hanging around."

"I go through hell to get out tonight and that's the best that you can come up with? Now that's lame!"

"C'mon, Charlie, your mum has got to know by now that you are getting too old to go, Zain's mum and dad go without him and my folks went through the same last year with me, but they get over it."

Zain looked on at the usual greetings of his two friends, the quick crossfire was standard practice, he knew they would stop in a moment and the conversation would swap to computer games, food, tv or girls instead so he just smiled and found a comfortable spot.

Zain and Charlie had met at pre-school and had been in the same class at school ever since. Their parents were now also good friends so they would always go out together at the weekend or be going to each other's house for dinner. Tommy, however, had moved up a few years ago from Norwich. His dad had got a new job in Matlock with the land registry and the only realistic option that they had was to move the whole family. It wasn't what Tommy had wanted to hear at the time having just started high school with all of his friends. The thought of moving and having to start afresh in a whole new part of the country was a bit daunting.

He had soon settled in though, having been sat with Charlie on his first day at his new school and from that day they had been friends ever since.

Crich, the village where they all now lived was high on the hills in Derbyshire, difficult to access by the tiny roads, which were often closed especially when the weather turned, and surrounded by moorland. The majority of the village was made up from local stone cottages which all fanned out from the market square. From the marketplace the village continued to climb upwards past the school and church before finally reaching the Memorial Tower and the Tramway museum which was built in an old open cast mine.

It wasn't exactly what every teenager had hoped for in a place to grow up. There was little to do in the evenings apart from the park. You could go to the local Scouts group once a week but the boys had all but stopped going towards the end of last year so that left them sitting in the market square. This though had caused a few problems as they liked to make a bit of noise as they sat chatting. It was after this that the boys had decided to move out away from the houses for some privacy. That's what they now said anyway, the truth as Tommy and Zain knew was that after Charlie had split up with his girlfriend Alison, he no longer wanted to see her out in the evenings and the park or the market square was where she usually went with her mates.

From their position on the far side of the valley the boys would have seen the procession coming over the hill tops had they been paying attention, however they had been sat on the Sitting Stone, each of them had found a stick and they were playing a game of 'flicky' which was now becoming competitive. They had started to tally up scores against each other. Tommy had named the game one evening a few months ago and had declared it a test of ultimate skill. At some point it was even possible he had decided that it should be introduced as a new sport to school and taught to every student across the country, only because he thought he was the best at it.

The boys were taking turns at flicking a smaller stick towards a target determined by their opponent and it had already whiled away a good hour.

"C'mon, Tommy! You're taking far too long. I think, new rule, number 27. You are only allowed fifteen seconds to line up and take your shot." Charlie was becoming frustrated at having to wait.

Tommy raised his eyebrows and gave a sideways glance at Charlie.

"Alright, fifteen seconds from now. Prepare to witness how a true master applies his skills!" He carefully placed the end of his stick under the smaller twig which lay on the floor in front of him. He had taken care not to place it too close to the start line which had been crudely scratched into the mud. His shoulders started to move up and down as his tongue slowly curled up over his top lip with concentration. His arm lurched suddenly propelling the twig skywards.

Charlie and Zain burst out laughing. "That was the most tragic thing I have ever witnessed, that has to be a minus point, what do you say, Zain?"

"Hey, now I got distracted look over there. We missed the first lot of people coming over the hill." Tommy stood up to get a better view of the line of candle lights that had been flowing across the ridge of the hill in front of them, for at least half an hour judging by the number of lights. "I know I don't like going but it is quite a spectacular view when you see it from a distance like this, bet it looks great from the other side of the valley."

Zain was nodding his head. "Well maybe we should all agree to go next year. We could go as a group. We'd have each other to talk to and our parents would be happy that we were getting involved."

"Do you know, Zain that is probably the best idea one of us has had tonight," replied Charlie.

With that the boys returned to playing their game each of them mulling over the idea of taking part in the procession again. Charlie only wished that they had come to this agreement earlier in the week, that would have saved him a whole load of grief.

It had just reached nine o'clock and the three boys had almost come to the decision to move on to the park, with some reluctance from Charlie, when they saw a dark coloured car pull up on the road below them. This had been the first bit of movement nearby that they had seen in the last couple of hours and it was unusual they thought as the road was seldom used by traffic. It was one of the reasons why they came to the Sitting Stone, people from the village rarely went there after dark so they had the place to themselves.

As they watched, both of the doors opened, and they could just about make out the shapes of two people moving around as they went to and fro in front of the car headlights. The men had gone to the boot of the car a couple of times and had taken out some sort of box which they had then in turn taken something from. It was a little hard to see exactly what was going on, but it had made the boys stop talking and they were now taking great interest in what the two men were actually doing.

A few minutes had passed by now and the men had continued to move around their car. They had started to look around with a torch and then they moved over to the side of the road by the wall farthest from the boys.

"What do you think that's all about then?" whispered Charlie as though he was stood right behind the two men.

"I don't know, mate, but I don't think they heard you," Tommy's short and sharp answer came back.

"Oh yeah." Charlie had realised it was pointless to whisper as there was no way they could be heard at that distance. "No, I mean why have they gone to the 'Merryweather Stone'? I know people like to go and see it, but I could think of better times to come, like when it's light to start with."

Charlie was right thought the others, many visitors who came to Crich walking would often take the short detour out of the village to come and see the Merryweather Stone. Everybody knew that it had been there for hundreds of years and was much older than the two stone walls that had been built up to it by the local landowners. At some point it had been carved but time had eroded it so badly that you could no longer make out what the picture was or what it had said. It stood at the side of Chadwick Nick where the lane cut down towards the canal, about one and a half metres tall and had a shallow dip on the top. Each of the two sides that were left visible had smoothed over indentations where the carvings had once been.

The boys continued to watch the two men as they ferreted around the side of the road. The men spent a few minutes looking at the Merryweather Stone and then moved back over towards their car looking up towards the village. Now and then one of them would make a hand gesture in the general direction of the village.

"Not being funny, but somebody else is coming now." Tommy pointed towards the top of the road where a set of headlights had come in to view over the brow of the hill. "Well that's even weirder, why have they stopped up there?"

The headlights that Tommy had spotted belonged to an old white van with green and white writing down the side, the shapes of the letters could just be made out in the faint moonlight. The van had come over the brow of the hill slowly and then stopped at the top. Its headlights were shining down the road towards the car that had been parked there for a good ten minutes now.

This new arrival had certainly made the first visitors change their mind about hanging around any longer. When the boys returned their gaze, the two men had already gotten back in to their car and had started the engine. The engine revved and a short spin of the wheels could be heard on the gravel that was down either sides of the road. This was all a new level of excitement for the boys as nothing like this ever happened in the village.

The van now made its way hesitantly down the hill towards the small layby where the first car had parked. It pulled over, its occupants unaware that they were being watched from afar with a keen interest.

"Look, that's a Burrowdale's van, what are they up to down there? This is all a bit odd to me given that car has just gone in such a hurry." Tommy spoke out catching the others by surprise as they had become fixated on what was unfolding before their eyes.

"Good grief, Tommy! Tell me next time you're thinking of scaring me, hey! Probably just came for the procession earlier," Charlie replied.

"That must be about finished for most people, they're just clearing up over there now you know that, besides they're going the wrong way."

"How do you know that they are going the wrong way and who are they anyway?"

"Well if you come down Chadwicks Nick Lane, that's this road, you might as well have stayed on the main road in to the village, and they're from Bonsall. Dad always goes on about them, oh and that means that they should have come from over there." Tommy had raised his arm to point out over the hill and along the valley in front of them.

"We went over there last year when we had to get his car seen to, do you remember when the lights kept switching on and off by themselves? He says it's the only local place he would trust with the Volvo."

"He calls them something else though, Burrowdales yes, but what does he call them? 'Hoarders', 'Heapers', 'Storers'… No, 'Keepers', that's what he said, don't know why but I recall him saying it: 'Taking the car to the keepers, wanna come with me?' Cool place they've got. A bit strange when you come to think about it though, for a garage it's packed full of stuff and I mean packed, more like an antiques shop than a garage."

Zain had half been listening to Tommy speaking but he had kept his eye on what was happening below.

"Well those two Burrowdale's men have just done exactly the same as the first two blokes, it wouldn't surprise me if they jumped in their van and sped off in a moment."

No sooner had the words come from Zain's mouth than the noise of the van doors could be heard slamming, the engine starting and the wheels spinning on the gravel. All three boys looked at each other with puzzlement on their faces. They had just been witnesses to one of the weirdest events they had seen in a long time, but what was unusual was that it didn't involve any one of them. It had certainly gained their interest and they all now had a desire to find out what was so exciting about the Merryweather Stone, especially this evening.

Tommy made the first stupid comment. "I know that we are currently snowed under with an abundance of things to do, but does anybody want to try and fit a little wander down to see what is so interesting over there?"

Zain gave Tommy a quick glance out of the corner of his eye and thought he would carry it on. "Well let me see, Tommy, if I could just consult with my diary, hmm, I could probably fit in an evening snack meeting to discuss, other than that I'm afraid I am exceptionally busy this evening. I have a lot of sitting on this cold hard rock to do." To add to his drama Zain had pulled out a chocolate bar and was offering it around to see if they would go for it.

They turned around expecting a comment from Charlie, however what they found was that he was already on his feet and was making his way down through the gorse bushes jigging side to side being careful not to get snagged on the thorns.

"C'mon we're off," said Zain.

"Strange folk in Derbyshire." The words came out of Tommy's mouth, but it wasn't clear to the others if he had meant to say it out aloud and they both gave him a look as if to imply who was he calling weird?

Chapter Two

The Procession of Lights (Friday)

"**M**um, are you OK?" called Jess from the top of the stairs.

"Yeah, it's OK, it's just your brother." Sally was standing in front of the mirror and had paused before answering. She looked up the stairs towards her daughter who was stood on the landing in full costume. A long black dress and white petty coat in homage to Florence Nightingale where the original inspiration for the lanterns used in the procession had stemmed. Sally felt a surge of pride seeing Jess standing there, hair neatly tied up in a bun, wiggling her lantern around, more importantly, honouring the family tradition.

Just because she had argued with Charlie it didn't mean that she should spoil the evening for Jess and herself. The shuttle busses would start running in the next ten minutes and it was always good to be there early in order to get a seat. She looked into the mirror and made one more adjustment to her eyeliner where the tears had smudged it. With that Sally decided that she would was good to go.

"Grab your things, Jess, we need to go and catch the bus and don't forget your hat and gloves it's going to be cold out there tonight."

Sally, Charlie, and Jess had taken part in the procession for as long as she could remember. They all had the costumes. 'It adds to the authenticity', Sally had told Charlie and Jess each time they came out of the box, even when they knew it was just because she liked to see them wearing it. Sally knew Charlie was growing up and she missed her little boy. The lanterns they used had also been handmade and she had spent quite a bit of time on them and she was proud, and always made sure that the others from the village noticed them too.

This was the first time that Charlie had not been. She had seen the slight regret in his eyes as he had left the house but she knew that he felt that he had done it enough times and there was no way she was going to let him hold one over on her having to do something for her sake. None of his friends had been for the last couple of years, they just made fun of him at school which he wouldn't have to go through this year. That was how he had justified it in their argument. Still, it was upsetting to her.

The procession tried to re-capture an event from 150 years earlier when the villagers had walked a similar route which ended up in the marketplace and all who had taken part had a tea party. The change to the evening was mainly due to the time of year that it could be done due to other events and by the council granting permission. It was due to this though that the idea came about to also incorporate the lanterns which made it unique from similar types of walks in the country. If you asked most of the participants, that was now their favourite part and the hard timers had all spent long hours working on their lanterns.

The walkers would congregate at Lea. Here everybody would wait until around 6:00pm as the sun was just starting to set, it was then that the lanterns played their part and gave full effect. To see the line of lights moving steadily along the lane was inspirational. There was no official start it just got underway when the first person knew it was right, this was a strange way but there had never been any arguments, and everybody would always wait until it was dark enough. The first person would start off down the hill towards Whatstandwell to where the canal joined, and the rest would follow. It was common knowledge though that the first person also known as 'The First', then had the responsibility of greeting each and everybody at the finishing line, that way it did not become and had never been a race.

From the point of the canal it was all uphill and was quite challenging, hang a left at the school and follow the road all the way twisting and turning until the gravel lane on the right was visible. Some people found this bit eerie as they had to leave the village through the woods, the trees of which overhung the lane making it feel claustrophobic. As the parade then left the woods, they would be able to see the Memorial Tower. Just another mile along the path through the fields and around the edge of the village. Here the police would cordon off the road to traffic in order to allow everybody to cross over. Reaching the driveway to the Memorial grounds was always good. The distinctive smell of food being cooked, fried onions, burgers and chips drifted through the air and as the crowd gathered the atmosphere became electric. So many people coming together in happiness and at a place where they could remember those who could not be with them made it even more of a special occasion, this is why, most of the village was there. Everybody knew everybody and anybody who was new could be identified straight away and they would usually be joined by one of the local villagers to guide them along.

This had been the preferred route since the day that Mr Pilcher opened the first procession over twenty-five years ago or so. As far as popularity went the procession had reached its height several years back when the newspapers had arrived along with the local news crew. Partly to report on the procession and a piece of modern-day history taking place but also because some T.V. celebrity had decided that they needed to promote themselves a little. He had been in most of the big soap operas, not massive parts, and he was from Buxton so he kind of made out like it was home.

———————

There was a steady mumbling of voices as people along the way were gently chatting about this and that. It was the informal atmosphere that was one of the aspects that gave the event such a relaxed feeling that and the gentle pace. It was just coming up to seven o'clock when Mrs Cooper and Jess had made it through the wooded gravel track and onto the open fields. This was one of their favourite moments, as it was here that they could see the whole procession spread out over the hills in front of them.

Mrs Cooper thought of her Charlie as she walked along by the stone wall at the side of the path and had a strange sense that he was looking out and watching her cross the field saying to his friends, 'Oh, here we go, lads, I can see the first of the lanterns coming over the brow of the hill, see it? That's my mum up at the front'. Her eyes started to fill up slightly with tears, but she didn't want to get upset. She knew that her Charlie was getting older, growing up and the time would always have come when he would not want to join her on these days, it was just that she had not expected it to be today. She was missing him. Her mind came back to focus on the tiny hand that she was holding in hers and remembered that Jess was still there with her. She would still make this a night of memories for her.

"C'mon, sweetheart I think when we get to the end of the walk, we should have a…" Sally paused for a moment and looked in to her daughter's eyes waiting for that moment of excitement. "Hot chocolate."

"Ooo, yes please, Mummy."

Jess had been great all night and she mustn't forget that, despite how annoyed she was with Charlie. They had reached a point in the field where the path had grown wide enough for others to pass so had decided to stop and watch the lights winding their way over the hill in front of them. 'The First' could be seen away in the distance next to the Memorial Tower. Mrs Cooper stood proudly with Jess, Charlie's sister, both dressed head to toe in their costumes that she had painstakingly made, each year adding more and more detail until they were the finished articles they wore today. There was a matching costume at home that had been made for Charlie, but it now just sat at the bottom of the suitcase where she kept them.

Oh, he is going to have to make this up to me, she thought.

"Charlie not here, Sally?" asked one of the passing neighbours.

"Oh, hello, Kylie, Ruby, no, er, no he had homework that he needed to get finished for tomorrow morning, you know how it is when they start getting close to their exams." She was slightly embarrassed by the fact that Charlie had not come down with them today but at the same time was glad, had he been there in the mood they parted earlier he would have spoilt the whole evening for them she thought.

"Oh, I see. Well, have you heard that there's talk of changing the route for next year?" Ruby, Mrs Spencer, was part of the village council and had been privy to the new information before the rest of the village and had now joined the conversation.

"No, dear no! Why would they do that?" Kylie wanted to catch up with Sally really but thought it polite to entertain Mrs Spencer.

"Well there hasn't really been a very good reason to date, but I hope that I can count on you to support the rest of us should we need to stand our ground and say no to the change."

Mrs Spencer was happy of the reinforcements as she saw it. "Well my husband told me it was to do with that new Councillor Burrowdale. It's all her idea, she says it would be more historically correct if we all came up the main road and over the Moor top. Ridiculous idea though, it is far too dangerous in the dark, oh I mean, and I've never even seen her here, I don't know who she thinks she is."

Sally was trying to be a little calmer about the situation as she had noticed that people were starting to pay attention to the outburst. "If it is the same woman, Mrs Spencer, I think she's only been in Crich about a year, hasn't she?"

"Yes, that's her, you'll find her round at the Cliffside pub later no doubt, they say her brothers go in there quite a lot, but only once every four weeks. They go in for a few nights and then they don't see them again till the next month. Bonsall folk, never met a sane one yet."

"Well we can't judge people like that, Mrs Spencer, not because of where they come from and I'm sure there are some lovely people in Bonsall."

They carried on walking and as they reached the entrance to the Memorial Tower the lights from all of the torches could be seen forming in to great circles around a small central platform. As the people walked it made the lights look as if they had all been drawn in towards this central spot like moths around a great flame.

Mr Pilcher was busying himself near to the main stand and was nipping here and there to see this person and that. It had long been known that he had had a great part in reviving and reorganising the event as he had a keen interest in keeping any tradition that had been part of the village going. He was currently speaking to Councillor Burrowdale, no doubt reminding her of names of people to mention in the speech that she was about to give. He took a few steps backwards and disappeared into the crowd of people that had gathered to the side of the small stage that had been erected for the evening. Councillor Burrowdale approached the microphone and the crowd started to silence.

"Good evening, Crich and guests. It is with great honour that I am able to stand here this evening having participated in one of Derbyshire's newest traditions. I may be new to the village but I feel that I have already been made to feel part of this community by all of those that I have met and tonight is a shining example of the openness and welcoming attitude that the people of Crich, Lea Holloway and Whatstandwell have. Personally, I believe that tonight has been a great evening and I have heard from those of you that have been doing this for many years that you are in agreement. It only remains for me to now say thank you on behalf of us all, to all of those who have helped out to ensure tonight has run smoothly and for keeping us safe and especially for those who have organised tonight's event. Now Mr Pilcher would not like me to do this but without his commitment to bring back this event I am sure that we would and could not all be stood here tonight. Thank you wherever you have now disappeared to, and I am being serious as he was stood right beside me a moment ago, please don't let him forget our gratitude."

There was a slight pause as people started to look around to see if Mr Pilcher was stood next to them, but he was nowhere to be seen. "Thank you all again for coming this evening and let us all enjoy the rest of the night. Thank you."

The crowd gave a round of applause and then began to move off into their little groups, visiting the stalls that were there, enjoying the warm food and drinks after their evening walk.

"Good grief she can lay it on a bit." Mrs Spencer was adamant that she was having none of it, this lady had upset her in some way, and she wasn't going to hear the last of it.

"Oh, Mrs Spencer let it be, c'mon. I promised Jess a hot chocolate, please won't you join us?" Sally spoke trying to take Mrs Spencer's mind off the subject.

The evening's events had gone superbly, and it only remained for the final few to make their way home or for some, to the differing pubs where the celebrations would be carried on until late into the evening. Sally knew that Jess would be tired and like many others made her way home to get changed and off to bed.

Chapter Three

Strange Goings On (Friday)

The evening was getting on and the steady flow of lights that had lit up the hill top earlier had long since stopped, the glow around the Tor fading as the rest of the village had finished their evening parade. The whole village would soon be theirs again and nobody would bother them as they took their stroll through the empty streets.

The boys had decided it was time to head on and set off for the park, by now the younger teenagers would have gone home so they could sit on the swings or go on the zip wire. The village took on a different feeling in the evening, it was eerie in that you would not see anybody else, but the boys found this somewhat comforting. Walking along the road the night light switched from hues of blue as the moon broke through the clouds and then in to oranges as they passed beneath the street lights. Every now and then they could hear the distant roar of a car on the main road far down in the valley as the sound was carried on the breeze. Other than this it was only their footsteps and voices that broke the evening silence.

The boys knew that there would be a few people who would have gone over to The Black Swan and the other pubs after the procession for a few drinks including their folks, but if they went down by Tommy's house they could cut through to the park. The boys came up Sandy Lane then cut across the sheep fields and went through the metal gate at the end of the row of houses. Tommy could see that his folks must be at home and were still up or at least the living room light had been left on.

This part of the village was made up of the old council houses, the streets were wide and tree lined, and the old-folks' houses on their right were well lit up as usual and the houses along the road all had their curtains drawn shut for the evening. What was different today was that up ahead the boys could see the black car that they had seen earlier in the evening parked at the side of the road. It stood out against the orange glow of the street lights which were reflecting back leaving bright white lines down its contours.

As they drew closer it became a lot clearer and Tommy was taking an interest in the BMW that was in front of him. He started to real off facts about the type of car he thought that it was, trying to prove his knowledge of cars to the other two, M5 this and 400bhp its 0-60 speed. They continued to walk on as Charlie and Zain began to make ridiculous suggestions about the car mocking Tommy for his interests.

Zain was slightly ahead of Charlie and Tommy as they lined up with the car, and he instinctively dipped his step as he walked to take a sneaky peek inside. He quickly straightened up and quickened his pace.

"Wow, there's somebody in it!"

They all tried to act as though this hadn't taken them aback, but it had caught them unawares as they were not expecting to see anybody. They walked past awkwardly trying to look casual as though they hadn't noticed and didn't care.

Tommy couldn't hold it in and chanced a look over his shoulder. He could clearly see that both of the occupants had stopped what they were doing and were now intently focused on the three boys. He quickly turned to face forward and hastened his pace slightly trying to catch up with Zain.

"I fink vey mighh ave votived ug," said Tommy out of the corner of his mouth.

"What?"

"I said I think they might have noticed us!"

"It's alright, Tommy, we're just going to the park we haven't done anything wrong. It's completely normal to check out someone who is sat in a car, especially round here. It's our village and we know they are not from here."

"Well, I tell you what, Charlie, you have a look to see if they are still watching us because they certainly didn't like me looking at them."

Charlie thought several times about what the consequences might be if he turned around and then remembered his own words, it was his village, he lived here, and he wanted to know who these strangers were. All this time the boys had been walking and had reached the corner of the road. It was the perfect opportunity to have a cheeky glance whilst pretending to see if the road was clear.

Charlie purposefully exaggerated his head movements looking first to the left and then to the right, bringing his gaze onto the car. The light inside was now on and unfortunately for Charlie he made direct eye contact with the men inside.

"Oh boy."

The words came out involuntarily from Charlie's mouth and even though he knew he should turn around, he couldn't stop looking. They had obviously been keeping an eye on them all the way down the road and they wanted the boys to know that they did not want any attention from pesky teenagers.

Charlie's head whipped straight around, "Keep walking and get to the park, quick, they're watching us."

The moment that their feet stepped from the path and hit the road they could hear the car engine start. They walked as quickly as they could without making it obvious that they were trying to get away. The car tyres hummed as they rolled slowly down the hill towards them.

Charlie could feel the backs of his legs starting to burn as he was walking a lot faster than he would usually. Tommy and Zain were right by his side, and he could hear Zain talking under his breath but could not quite make out what he was saying. A few more metres and they would be near enough to the old railway archway that spanned the footpath and then they could start to run. The car wouldn't be able to follow them from that point. The boys could hear the car getting closer. That was it, far enough.

"Run!" shouted Charlie.

The boys set off like they had just started the hundred metre race at the Olympics. Charlie did not know if it was because he was running or whether the wind had changed direction as a sudden gust was in his face, he could feel it blowing through his hair. The sound of their footsteps crunched on the gravel and echoed as they went underneath the tunnel. They pelted down the dark path dodging the overhanging branches so as not to cut their faces. Tommy and Charlie spun their heads back at the same time to see if they were being followed and nearly fell over each other.

"Wait up wait up!" Charlie slowed down and then stopped, ducking down to look under and through the branches. He could not see anyone on the path behind them but he was still half expecting the two men to come bounding around the corner any second. His heart was pounding, and he realised how unfit he must be as that short sprint had taken it out of him.

"I can hear the car. It's heading off back down the road," Tommy called to Charlie.

Charlie was thankful for the news from his friend. He took a few steps back towards Tommy and looked across the playing field in the direction of the car noise which seemed to be coming from behind the row of houses that surrounded the park. He turned to look at Tommy then squinted his eyes to look closer at Tommy's face.

"Are you sweating, mate?" Charlie asked with a smirk on his face.

Tommy wiped his hand across his forehead and took away the beads of sweat that had formed.

"Might be but that's only because it's warm tonight." He knew it wasn't warm, but he had to save face.

They both looked around to check on Zain, now that they felt slightly safer.

'The old railway bridge'

Zain however had in his wisdom chosen not to stop and thought the further he got away the better. He had continued running and was well up the path near where the park opened out to the shared garages. He took a quick look around to see if his schoolfriends were there, but they must have all gone home as the park was empty. The quietness suddenly hit him, and he realised that he was alone, and his mates had stopped down the path. He noticed that his chest was moving heavily, and the back of his throat was burning with the cold air as he breathed in.

That must be the fastest I've ever moved, he thought as he scanned through the darkness trying to keep eyes on his friends. Tommy and Charlie slowly turned towards him and started to walk in his direction. Walking was good in his mind; it must mean that nobody had followed them.

They gathered together. "What the hell was that all about, that's straight out of Psycho land, all we did was look in to the car," Zain commented.

"Yeah, well let's lay low and try not to go near them again, some people like their privacy." Charlie had not enjoyed his little run.

"Hang on here a second we can just see through the houses to the market square. Look the headlights, that must be them. It turned towards Fritchley; see they've gone."

"Yeah, well I really don't feel like seeing them again tonight. Thanks, Tommy. C'mon, if we go up towards Cromford Road we should be good."

They gave it a few minutes and then as a team decided that it was safe to move on. On hindsight they should have gone across to Zain's house which backed onto the park, but the night was still young, and they didn't want to head in yet so the plan to head around the village for a stroll still stood.

Zain had gone out in front again, only just, but it was like he had volunteered to take point, either that or he knew it was always the one at the back who got grabbed.

Clever lad, thought Charlie as he checked over his shoulder one more time feeling slightly paranoid about being followed.

The path stopped at the shared garages and then started again on the other side where it cut through between the gardens of the houses to meet up with the side road that would lead them up to the church. Zain had reached the steps and the others were still several metres behind him now mainly due to them continually checking around to make sure nobody else was near. Without knowing it they were quite shook up by what had just happened as this was out of the ordinary and the adrenalin was still running through them.

The next few seconds happened in slow motion, or at least that's what it felt like. Tommy and Charlie were catching up with Zain when they watched him suddenly dive to the floor, landing on the steps like a sack of spuds. Nature controlled their motions and they ducked down to conceal themselves slightly. Charlie's eyes moved upwards keeping an eye on Zain as his own body moved towards the floor. His hands hit the ground hard and he felt the gravel dig into his palms and fingertips. His face grimaced with the sharp pain. Zain was still hugging the floor. Tommy was on the floor too with what Charlie could only think must have been the same expression on his face as what he was pulling.

It was only now he understood Zain's actions. At the top of the steps in front of them two cars were parked which had obscured most of the view for Zain up or down the road until he had reached the very top. It was here that Zain had seen the oncoming danger and taken action. Charlie watched the black car roll past the top of the steps slowly. Its headlights had been switched off to make it less conspicuous.

He reached out and gave Tommy a good shove on his shoulder and sent him rolling over the embankment that surrounded the playground. There was a muffled grunt and groan as he reached the bottom. Charlie was hoping that Tommy would not react and give them away. He could see that Zain was out of sight, Tommy was dealt with just him. He spun on his heal, his shoulders twisted backwards and from what he could recall there was a low hedge not far behind him that would soften his fall.

There it was. The bush reached around, cushioning him as he fell in to it. To him the rustling of the leaves was incredibly loud but that's because the branches were now brushing past his ears and slapping him across his face as they tried to form back into shape. Charlie lay, stiff as a board, motionless for what seemed an eternity half suspended in the air by the bush. His mind had moved focus to the car. He could no longer see up the path, but he was unsure if he could be seen in the opposite direction. He checked down his body and could see that his feet, although motionless were clearly in the street light.

Slowly he edged them inwards knowing that a sudden movement could draw attention to himself and Zain was closer still on the steps, he presumed.

"It's all clear," came a whispered voice.

It was Zain who had now crawled up the steps and was lying flat on his belly, peering underneath the parked cars. He was making hand gestures beckoning them to come towards him. Tommy's hand reached out and grabbed Charlie who was still dazed.

"C'mon, let's go and see what's happening."

Tommy helped pull Charlie to his feet and they both looked down at the hedge where Charlie had previously been lodged.

"Ooo, don't think they're going to be happy with that, mate!" Tommy was sometimes the master of the understatement.

"Well there wasn't much that I could do and, well there isn't time to sort it out now! We can always come back tomorrow and try and… I don't even know how you would fix it. Do you plump a bush up?"

"Tommy, Charlie." Zain was calling them over again. He was still laying on the floor, his head, however, was moving from left to right scouting out the road either side of them.

"They've gone down there and it looks like they are turning around, yep get down."

The boys now all lay next to each other on the steps. They could hear the sound of the car engine gently running as it came close. From where they were lying, they could take advantage of the fact that they could see underneath the car in front of them, but they were well hidden from sight. They watched the alloy wheels roll past and felt a sense of relief that it had not stopped. They continued to watch the car move further up the road and eventually around the corner.

Again, the boys could hear the engine rev and pull off from the junction and to them it sounded as if the car went back in towards the main village.

"That's it, they've gone," said Zain.

"Well we thought that a few moments ago and that turned out to be a real shocker when they came down the road. Let's not have that again." Charlie's point was a good one and both Zain and Tommy knew it.

"Couple of freaks if you ask me though, why would you drive around with your headlights off looking for three kids?"

"Beats me, Zain but I suggest that we go through 'The Scotts'." This was the name of the area around this edge of the village. "We can head over to the Tramway museum for a bit, can't really get much further away from the village centre and we should be able to hear them coming down the road if they come back."

Chapter Four

The Waving Light, Way Past Bedtime (Friday)

The boys had decided to take the lane out around the eastern edge of the village and up towards the Tramway museum for a final patrol before they headed on home. This was better than going back the way they had come past the guys in their car who they had just watched driving off in the opposite direction. On this side of the village the boys were given fantastic views to the valley and rolling hills of the Peaks. Charlie liked it at night, how the hills appeared to be layered on top of each other as the differing shades of bluey grey faded into the distance. And there alone on the far hill the dark shadow of Riber Castle could also be found.

Tommy had planned to stay at Charlie's house that evening so he didn't need to be home. Tommy's parents were fine with both staying out until eleven, so as long as they were back by then it would all be good. Zain's parents had also given him to this time but only at the weekends and as long as he was with his two friends.

As they came to the end of the dirt track another side road joined the main road that led out of Crich and down towards Lea Holloway. The only buildings further out of the village from them now were the Cliff Side pub and the barn that was used by the furniture maker.

"Looks busy," commented Zain as he looked over at the pub.

Due to the number of visitors and that most of the village had been at the procession earlier, the pubs had seen an increase in their usual clients for the evening. Voices could be heard from the yard at the front of the pub as the occupants had spilled outside and were now enjoying their last drinks of the evening.

The boys lined up at the junction of the roads. Charlie stepped forward and turned to face them. "Well, well, lads it looks like our Burrowdale friends from earlier are here. This may sound completely insane, but do you want to have a look in through that van window to see if anybody is in it?" Charlie joked with Tommy.

"Yeah, I reckon that van has a 3.6 litre engine, Charlie and can do 0-60 in 5.6 seconds." Zain had twigged onto Charlie's lead and knew that if he pushed, Tommy would bite and would not be able to resist going to have a look despite what had happened the last time that he looked in to a car window.

Tommy was already crossing the road, his head shifting around making sure not to be seen from the pub terrace.

"He is proper stupid sometimes I swear," said Zain as they started to follow at a distance. At the same time, he and Charlie were both ready to turn and run.

The van was parked in the layby on the opposite side of the road to the pub. A number of other cars were also parked up. This was usual for patrons of the pub who travelled from the nearby villages to spend the evening, today more so with the number of visitors to the village. Tommy had reached the back of the van and was trying to be cunning by looking into the mirrors to see if he could see into the cabin that way. It was clear that he was having no luck as he continued to move closer. He turned and placed his back to the side of the van and sidestepped down towards the driver's door. He paused.

His head twitched forwards quickly to look in and then he came pelting up the road towards Charlie and Zain. The boys turned and began to run too as Tommy called them.

"Joke, I'm joking, there's nobody in it."

The boys all stopped and took some deep breaths.

'Tramway museum'

"I think I just wet myself."

"That is far too much information thanks, Zain," said Charlie as he looked uncomfortably at his friend.

"Well they must be in the pub. See, we are reading too much into all of this. They are just a couple of blokes who have come over from Bonsall. Hey, they may even live here for all we know."

Tommy was right and it had been a long evening with lots going on, more than what they would usually fit in to a whole year. They had now reached the front gates of the Tramway museum, around the corner from the pub and were standing by the railings, talking about the old car that they could see that was parked halfway down the park. Charlie had climbed up on to the wall on one side of the large ornamental gateway that fronted the museum and was sat on the top. Tommy was making his way up on the opposite side while Zain had opted to chill out below, leaning back against the gates themselves.

"I love this place! The museum. I know that sounds weird but there's something about it especially when you are in there. That feeling of nostalgia, I can sometimes really feel like I am back 'int' good old days." Tommy tried to add a strong Yorkshire accent to make it sound even older, but failed tragically, sounding more Australian to his friends.

"Yeah alright, Tommy." Zain was now having none of it as he had known Tommy long enough and well enough to know that he did not like history in the least.

What he did know was that all three of them enjoyed being out in the village late at night. That was a certain. There was a silence that could not be described other than comforting. Yes, they could hear the odd car on the main road in the valley but this was only if the wind blew in the right direction, maybe a plane would go over once in a while but very rarely and other than this it was the sound of nature. They would often be able to hear a bird cry out; they never knew what it was, but it was always there at some point in the night.

Now that the village had gone quiet, they were starting to relax a little more and had been chatting for a good twenty minutes when they had come to the conclusion that nothing else was going to happen that evening. Zain threw the stone that he had in his hand away and watched it roll along the path. He leapt up from his lowly perch and looked up and down the road.

"Yep, it's all quiet, chaps, shall we head home?"

Charlie and Tommy were in agreement with Zain's summary. They could have sat there all night and the next person or thing they would see would be the first person on their way to work or the cyclists that usually came through early in the morning. On this note they all set off on the short journey towards the village centre.

As they reached the corner a voice came out from across the road "Evening, boys."

The boys were a little startled until they realised that it was Mr Pilcher. "Oh, evening, Mr Pilcher, pub close early?" Tommy had replied for the group. They would often see Mr Pilcher around the village and especially late on, usually around closing time for The Black Swan if they had thought about it more.

Mr Pilcher was well known around the village, he would help out on nearly every aspect of village life, any event that was happening he would be doing something. If the church had an event running, he would be there doing his part. Any problems happening in the village and you could guarantee he would always be the one that people could ask, and he would know what was going on or what to do. Oh, and he also knew everybody's parents. Which meant is was a good idea to be polite and kind to him.

The boys had never really worked out how old Mr Pilcher was, they knew that he had retired but he was still fit and active and despite having his grey, wispy hair there was an air and energy about him that filled him with a youthful happiness.

"Well it's been a busy old night, hasn't it?" Mr Pilcher didn't pause to give them a chance to answer. "The procession went as well as planned and it looked like everybody had a good time, wrapped up early though so most people are just having a last drink in the pub now. Noticed you weren't there this year."

The boys all looked at him with guilty faces, but they knew he couldn't be that good, or could he? Yes, he was right about them not being there this evening, but it was like he knew something else. What had happened to them was a couple of hours ago if that, gossip could not go that quickly, could it?

"Oh, you don't need to answer, I can see you all look tired. Now you boys be careful tonight there are some rum folk about and it's getting late. We've had a car racing up and down the high street earlier, didn't seem to care if they hurt anybody. If you see a black BMW, you get the number plate and let me know, would you?"

"We will, Mr Pilcher, just heading on home now though as it happens and you're right there are some strange folk around tonight, think that car came past us earlier tonight too over by Sandy Lane. You be careful on your way home too."

As Tommy was engaged in the conversation with Mr Pilcher, Charlie had been gazing around the hillside behind Mr Pilcher. Charlie's eyes opened about as wide as they could with astonishment as he saw the two torchlights flash across the top of the War Memorial in the distance. He soon realised that if anybody looked at him, he would have to explain what he had seen and with Mr Pilcher present he might as well wake up the whole village. He wiped the expression from his face as quickly as he could and looked at Mr Pilcher to see if he had noticed. He was still focused on Tommy, thankfully the few beers that they could smell on him were helping them. Must have numbed his senses slightly.

"Sorry to interrupt you, Mr Pilcher, but my mum is expecting me home soon so we need to be on our way sharpish if you know what I mean?" Charlie was desperate to speak to his friends so tried to tie the conversation up.

"Yes, you're right, young man, I shouldn't keep you standing around. You be on your way and take care."

"Thanks, Mr Pilcher," they all chimed in.

They turned around and started to walk down the road again while Mr Pilcher had also continued on his journey again. He was already at the main junction and heading off out of the village towards his home about half a mile away, when Charlie stopped the other two.

"Listen, while you were talking to Mr Pilcher I was looking up at the Tor and these great big lights came swinging across and lit it up! There has to be someone up there doing something they shouldn't. I know it's been a crazy one, but I need to know what's going on up there."

"I'm with you, Charlie, besides Pilcher just told us that the whole thing had finished early and everybody else is now in the pub or at home," came back Tommy.

"C'mon, why not, but if we see that car again and those blokes, I am straight out of there do you understand?" It was easy to tell that Zain was being serious as the tone in his voice had changed. The run in earlier had gotten to him.

"No, that's agreed, I'm not that interested in getting chased all the way home. We keep it quiet, creep up, have a quick look and then head on home. Deal, Zain?"

"Deal," Zain replied reluctantly.

They wanted to go up to the War Memorial to see what the lights were all about. With everybody gone by now, they knew something interesting was occurring and they needed to see it, but having told Mr Pilcher they were going home it meant it was going to be difficult. He had just gone in the exact direction that they needed to go.

The boys made their way along the street, but they deliberately walked as slowly as they could, every now and then checking to see if Mr Pilcher had gone far enough away. They could see the shadow of his head bobble past the hedge; that was it, he was around the next corner and out of sight. They turned around and crossed over the road to use the stone wall as cover, crouching down so as not to be seen. They took their time moving along the wall right up to the junction where Mr Pilcher had turned; there was still a chance that Mr Pilcher had stopped along the road on his way home.

Tommy took a quick look up the road and could see that it was completely clear, for now. They clambered over the wall and slid silently into the next field and through a gap in the hedge on the opposite side of the road. They were confident that this would help to conceal them from Mr Pilcher should he come back or glance over his shoulder a little farther down the lane. It was also a good way to be sure of not being seen from any other prying eyes. The path on the edge of the field led all the way up to the entrance of the War Memorial so it was the best route that they could think of. As they reached the kissing gate, they stopped once more to check up the road.

Zain, again, had taken to the front and given his actions earlier, Tommy and Charlie were happy to hang back slightly, but this time they were alert and looking and listening for anything out of the ordinary. They were about to move when Charlie reached out and grabbed Zain's shoulder to stop him stepping out.

"Look! Back up there."

Charlie was pointing with his left arm along the side of the hedge and up the hill. The boys all paused to look at what Charlie was pointing at. For a number of seconds there was nothing. Tommy was beginning to think that Charlie was making it up to continue to add excitement to their little adventure and then there it was.

A bright shaft of light streaked across the sky ahead of them, spun around dancing on and off of the low clouds above their heads and vanished again.

Chapter Five

A Bit Too Close (Friday)

The boys slowly crept through the gateway in the hedge at the foot of the driveway leading up to the Tor. They could now see the Memorial Tower standing proud on the hill top silhouetted by the last of the late evening moonlight before the moon disappeared behind the large blanket of cloud. The darkness which had come across them suddenly felt heavy. The Tower was taller than all of the houses in the village and when open it was possible to climb up the staircase inside to the viewing platform at the top. In the darkness, it was now only just visible to them.

As they drew closer to their intended target, they could see the outline of the two men standing next to their car; it was the same car that they had seen by the Merryweather Stone and in the village by the park earlier in the evening. This could surely not be a good thing thought Charlie. The men were oblivious to their presence, at the moment, and appeared to be in the middle of a heated argument.

The boys moved silently along the side of the hedge and made their way as close as they dare. "Here, get down behind the wall. They shouldn't be able to see us here, but we might be able to hear what they are saying."

Tommy crawled closer towards the low wall which ran around the edge of the memorial area. He paused mid crawl and turned towards Charlie.

"You're not going to like this but it's definitely those two folk from earlier."

As the boys got into position the moon broke out from behind the clouds suddenly casting a blue light around them. They lay still hoping that they couldn't be seen. Tommy slowly peeked around the edge of the wall. He could now see that the taller of the two men had dropped to his knees and was frantically sifting through the grass with his hands. He periodically looked up at the other and shook his head.

The grumbling and mumbling went on, but it was too faint for them to hear any exact words. But they knew from the tone that neither of them were happy at the situation they were currently in.

This went on for a few minutes until the clouds covered the moon again. Tommy could still just about make out the two men shuffling around. The shorter of the two had now stopped, however, and was peering keenly into the darkness around him. Every now and then he looked directly at Tommy. Tommy was half expecting him to call out or come running towards them shouting and screaming so was getting ready to run.

"Evening, gentlemen." The voice came booming from the darkness behind the boys. They froze. Charlie could see that Zain was starting to panic so he carefully reached out trying not to break their cover and put his hand on his arm to calm him. He knew that they were in a slight dip and they could not be seen from down the road. A bright beam of torchlight shone through the darkness and landed bang on the two men.

"Oh, evening officers, how are you today?"

"Thought that the whole event had wrapped up by now, gentlemen, any reason why you are up here this late?"

The police officers stepped closer, with their focus on the two men, they walked straight past the boys who were still huddled together on the ground, a small mound of grass to the side of them and the retaining wall in front of them.

"Yes, you're right, officers, well we left along with everybody else and it was only when we got in to town that I realised I had lost my wallet.

This was the last place that I had used it when I bought a coffee from the stall, so we came back to have a look and lo and behold it was just here by the side of the road."

The man reached into his trouser pockets and slowly pulled out a small leather wallet. The second man was remaining still and quiet letting his partner do all of the explaining.

"Guess I was lucky hey, but yep we can be on our way now if that's okay with you?"

"If you have found everything you have lost then it might be a good idea to be on your way home. May I remind you gentlemen that the memorial is closed to the public at night-time, so if anything like this happens again perhaps you could wait until first thing in the morning?"

"That's a good suggestion, officers, you know it would have been easier to find it in the daylight too. Thank you then, officers."

The two men briskly walked over to their car and climbed in, all the time the officers were watching, their torchlights moving around to check the ground and surrounding area. Again, the boys had luck on their side as the officers were facing away from them and their focus was on the two men now in their car.

As the BMW with its two occupants drove by, the nearest officer to the boys reached to his shoulder and called in to the station to let them know that they had finished up there and that they would be getting back to their patrol of the local villages. The police officers turned and walked back down the hill to where they must have parked their patrol car. As the sound of the officer chatting into his radio was getting fainter the boys began to relax again. They knew that they must be well out of sight now but lay still for a few more minutes just to make sure not to be caught.

"Good grief, how did they miss us, they must have walked within a couple of metres of us and they didn't see us!" Tommy was gobsmacked at their luck.

"Well it is pretty dark up here, it's probably the same reasons those blokes couldn't see us even when they were looking straight at us."

"Well it's freaked me out a bit alright, let's just keep an eye out in case they come back."

Tommy started to make his way over the small wall that they had been laying behind and headed over towards the spot where the men had been standing. He was keen to have a look around and see if he could make sense of what they had been up to. As the other two looked on, glancing round nervously to see if anybody else was coming, Tommy started to pace along the spot where the men had been looking.

"What can you see?" Zain whispered.

"Nothing, it's dark!" Tommy called back slightly louder than Zain had been comfortable with.

"He's not that bright, is he?" Charlie commented to Zain.

"Tommy, quiet, man, somebody might hear you!" Zain whispered more vigorously.

Tommy sat down by the side of the path. "Sorry, Zain, I guess you're right, besides I don't even know what we're looking for over here, the guy said he had found his wallet. It's just a path here, some grass over there a few rocks and gravel and a bit of rubbish left over from earlier. It doesn't make sense though. Why would they be up here after everybody else has gone and why say that they were here to the police because we know that they were on the other side of the village busy chasing us? I know we're up here now, but we're teenagers and this is what we do around here for entertainment."

Charlie and Zain made their way over and had sat next to Tommy.

"It's alright, chap, what did you think you was going to find, a key, money or something?"

Tommy did not reply, he sat with his head down between his knees. Charlie thought that his friend was looking tired and he too was beginning to feel the drain of the evening and a bit fed up on top. It had now definitely been a long evening nobody could deny it. Two encounters that had got their adrenalin pumping which was now running out. Charlie could feel his body beginning to tire and his thoughts had turned to climbing in to a warm bed and going to sleep.

Charlie reclined backwards and reached his arm around behind his head to create a sort of pillow to rest on. As he moved his hand his fingers brushed against a small stone. He gripped it into his fingers and started to roll it around in his hand. Tommy had begun to talk but Charlie's mind was now focused on what was in his hand.

That's unusual, he thought as his finger and thumb moved backwards and forwards over the stone. He could feel the grooves running over the surface but couldn't make it out as a shape, number or letter that he knew.

Charlie brought his arm back around and sat up lifting the stone closer to his face in order to get a clear look at what he had picked up. The stone was dark, too dark to look at, but it glistened in what light that they had. He could now just about make out the grooves that he had been rubbing his fingers over. He could clearly make out a pattern, but it wasn't anything he had seen before.

"Not being funny, lads but I think I know what they were looking for." Charlie now realised that he had been sat there for quite some time moving the stone around in his hand and Tommy and Zain had been chatting on. They both looked at him with expectation.

Charlie held out his arm and opened his hand to reveal the stone. "What is it?" asked Zain.

"It's some sort of stone but it's got this mark carved in to it, look." Charlie passed the stone over to Zain and he did exactly the same as Charlie. First rolling the stone around in his fingers then lifting it close to his face.

"Yeah, I can see why you would think somebody might be looking for it. It's not the typical sort of thing you leave lying around is it?"

Tommy reached over and took the stone out of Zain's hand. "Give it here it's probably some kind of kid's toy." He stopped sharply as soon as his hand came into contact with the stone. He knew straight away, he didn't know how, but he knew that it was not a toy. "You're right, Charlie, this is it. It must be important but that doesn't explain why they were up here late at night."

If Tommy and Charlie could have seen Zain's face, fully, they would have seen the moment the next thought had popped in to his head. A sudden fear had come over him and it was clear from the expression on his face. "You know earlier how we saw that car pull up and then the Burrowdale men arrived shortly afterwards and then we have had those two guys up here again? Well what if this belongs to them? I mean not to be funny, but they didn't look too friendly, you said that yourself!"

Tommy found himself nodding and was coming on board with what Zain was suggesting. Having thought back on the events that they had witnessed earlier at their Sitting Stone it started to fit in to place. Two guys in a car pulling up then moving on quickly, the Burrowdale men pulling up afterwards, the activities just now and the way they behaved when the police arrived. The realisation was that if the stone did belong to them, then they lied to the police and that means that they would not be far away waiting to return when it was safe for them to do so. The boys had to move and quickly.

Look it's getting late and I don't fancy running in to anybody else to..." Charlie stopped suddenly again. His head spun to the left and sure enough there at the bottom of the driveway to the Tor he spotted it. They hadn't noticed but the Burrowdale's van had pulled up and there was some sort of motion in the shadows around its side.

"Move it, move, they're coming now!" There was a distinct panic in Charlie's voice.

Tommy was on it and gave the instruction, "Crawl over to the wall, we'll head through the field."

With that the three boys did their best commando style crawl that they could, each was trying to stay as low as possible but also move as fast as they could. None of them wanted to be at the back for fear of being grabbed. Charlie was getting anxious now as this was all getting too weird for his liking.

This is Crich, this doesn't happen here, he thought.

They reached the safety of the field and paused to get their breath back. Tommy again was the one who found the courage to peek over and around the edge of the wall.

"I'm being serious now, those guys are coming up here and they are getting close, where's that stone?"

Charlie's hand moved directly to his left jacket pocket. The stone was there. "It's here in my jacket pocket, don't worry it's not going to fall out."

Their escape route was clear in Tommy's mind, across the field back to the main road, then they would be able to see the van. Anybody on the road would also be visible to them, they could then head down the path around the back of the church, drop Zain off and then around to his house. Even though Charlie was the main spokesman for the group at school and out with their other friends, when it came to these situations, planning in the instance was Tommy's skill and he had now taken charge of the group.

"Wait, Tommy, you take it, I don't want it on me or at home, it's freaking me out." Charlie had blurted this out as Tommy was about to explain his route home. Charlie was becoming overwhelmed by the thought of the strangers that were now coming into his life without invitation and he was not able to control it.

"Give it here quickly, we need to move. Head down the field towards the road, wait at the wall and if it is clear we are on our way to drop Zain off."

"I like the sound of that," Zain chirped up.

Charlie was already going through his pocket trying to grasp hold of the stone which kept falling through his fingers. Finally, he had a good grip and took it out, passing it quickly to Tommy.

The boys did not wait any longer and they were on their way. Upon reaching the wall they could see the figures up by the Memorial Tower around the area which they had been sat moments earlier. It was fine for them to move on. If they were quick about it, they could be down the road before the Burrowdale men could be back to their van. Two or three more minutes and they could be back at Zain's house.

As they met with the road, they knew it was time to run. It started as a quick sprint but after a few hundred metres they had slowed to a jog.

"There's my house, I'm going straight in, get gone and don't hang around. I'll see you tomorrow, my house for dinner remember, dad's cooking curry."

As Zain said night to Tommy and Charlie, Tommy gave Zain a reassuring look and gave his jacket pocket a tap to let him know the stone was there. Zain was off and towards the back gate to his garden.

"See you later, Zain, it's been epic. Come on, chappie, let's get back to mine. I believe in times like these I should say that we could do with a cup of tea, eh, Charles?"

———————

The room was dark apart from the gentle flicker of light coming from a number of candles that had been placed around the room. It had been a long night for its occupant and he now needed to know all of the events and if it was to be so, discover the outcomes of those events.

The man unscrewed a bottle of red wine and poured a glass. He returned the bottle to the side of the room and placed it on the floor by the wall. Walking over towards the table he took a long and steady sip of the drink from his glass. The man grabbed the back of the wooden chair and dragged it over to the table that was in the middle of the room. Apart from these two pieces of furniture and an old phone fastened to the wall, the room was bare. The curtains had been drawn closed on the windows that were on either side of the room, one facing east the other facing west, to prevent prying eyes from seeing the actions that were about to take place.

He opened a drawer at the front of the table, took out a small leather bag and placed it onto the table in front of him. He carefully untied the leather straps from around its neck and poured the contents gently on to the table. Before him now lay 24 stones. Circular in shape some of them appeared to be engraved with patterns. He cast his hands over them and touched each of them one by one as his hands moved gently across them.

He checked his watch and knew that the time was nearly upon him.

The man stood up, walked over to the curtains and opened the ones facing east. He had waited up especially for this moment. From his front room window there were views all the way across the Amber Valley and down towards the city of Derby a good twelve miles away. The first rays of sunlight were now coming over the horizon. This was the time.

He opened the drawer again and took out a small tablecloth. He placed the white cloth on to the table and rotated it to give him the correct direction. It was important for him to be facing the sun and to know which way the rune stones had fallen.

He lifted the stones into his hands and threw them down towards the table, over the cloth. His hands moved quickly dismissing all of those that were faced downwards. Only four runes remained on the table. He pulled them into the centre of the cloth and lined them up how they had fallen from left to right.

"Interesting, perhaps it is to be."

He cast his eyes up towards the rising sun and then shielded them from the bright rays, squinting slightly.

"Othala, Ehwaz, Algiz and Thurisaz. Well they shall definitely find companionship and danger."

Chapter Six

The Next Morning (Saturday)

Tommy had not slept well that night. A slight panic had come over him whilst lying in bed which had made it difficult to fall asleep. His dreams had tormented him, first he had seen swirls of carved stones, the writing spiralling round and round combined with a sense of falling down a deep dark hole. His next dream was that of being followed, never quite seeing any faces but knowing that somebody was there, watching, bright red eyes glowing through a mist and a smell, a stench that was most foul.

He had woken to the sound of hard rain hitting against his window. He sat up and drew the curtains back tucking the bottoms around the ends of his radiator to stop them closing again. It was usually a stunning view over the fields which he especially liked during the summer, however today the clouds were hanging low over the distant hills and a light mist had formed in the valley down by the river.

He reached over the edge of his bed and lifted his jumper from the floor at the foot of his bed where he had taken to leaving his clothes, much to his mum's despair. He could feel the difference in weight to usual knowing that in his pocket was the stone marked with the carved shape that they had found last night.

Tommy apprehensively reached into his pocket and touched the stone with his fingertips. He paused and looked out of his window again. With the dreams still vivid and the events of last night clear in his mind he could have sworn that he was being watched but that was nonsense he thought. Nobody knew they were there last night. Not at the Tor anyway. Yes, they had been seen by those guys in the car and the Burrowdale men possibly, and even if they were in fact looking for the stone, they couldn't have known it was here in Tommy's hand.

When his focus returned, he realised he was grasping the stone tightly and did not want to let go. He forced his fingers to open and gazed upon it. It was oval in shape and around five centimetres in length. The stone was perfectly smoothed off apart from where it had been carved but even these lines were smooth to the touch as if worn by time. Black would not have been the word to describe how dark the stone was, it was as if the light was absorbed by it, which made it difficult for Tommy to focus his eyes.

Tommy realised what he was looking at and was now intrigued by the rune symbol itself, almost like a kite with two tails he thought, running lengthways along the stone. The reverse side, however, was plain, not even a scratch. He had seen runes before but couldn't recognise them enough to say where it was from; cartoons and comic books were not always the most educational source when it came to fine details like that. Tommy did, however, recall there being a book somewhere downstairs that he had used once or twice for his homework.

Tommy looked over the other side of his bed. Sure enough Charlie was there all tucked up, curled around into a tight ball like a hamster. Seeing his friend made it all the more real. It was good that he was here, but it meant that everything that went on last night really happened. Tommy got that feeling again that he was being watched and he made one more look out of his window. He fixed on the wall at the far end of the field. His eyes followed the line of the wall moving in and out around the treeline. Did that bush just move? No, don't be daft. He was now a little happier in the knowledge that if there had been somebody there, he could not see them, or they had gone.

Again, the thought passed over his mind, *Nobody saw us, they don't know we have it. Anyway, to stand out there in this rain you would have to be mad.*

He made the decision to let Charlie sleep knowing that he would be tired, and he crept out of his room and made his way downstairs in to the dining room to find the book he was after.

The dining room was dark apart from a small line of light that was coming through around the edge of the blinds. The heating had kicked in and had made the room toasty warm. Tommy flicked the light on rather than opening the blinds. He was trying to recall the book and had a vague recollection of its appearance with a red and grey cover and a picture of a castle on the front.

He made his way over to the bookshelf and started to move his hands across the books reading the titles in his head to see if any of them jogged a memory. When that didn't work he went back to the beginning again and just started to look for a book that was red and grey. There on the third shelf down he saw a large book that fit the description. He pulled it from the shelf and went and sat down on the armchair in the corner of the room.

Tommy turned the book over and there was the picture of the castle. *Bingo!* he thought and started to flick through the pages to find the section on runes. As he turned the pages images of different periods of time throughout the history of England were passing by and the images were coming back to him. At some point he must have spent a lot of time looking at them to recall them but where was the section he needed?

He flicked the pages again and stopped nearer to the front this time and sure enough he had found roughly the right section. He skimmed across the text on the page picking out key words: "Rune, rune, rune where is it?" Tommy realised that he was becoming agitated about not being able to find what he wanted. He turned to the next page. *Yes*, he thought, *got you*. Tommy started to read more carefully what was being said about the use of rune stones and that was it, one paragraph.

"No, what does it mean? That is the most useless book in the world."

Tommy made his way back upstairs and returned to his room. He opened the door slowly so as not to bash it into Charlie's feet. To his surprise they were not in the doorway. He poked his head around the door to find Charlie sat up leaning against the side of his cupboard and staring out of the window.

"Morning, mate." Tommy spoke softly so as not to wake the others in the house.

"Morning, Tommy. Sleep well?"

"Not really no but hey, look!" Tommy tossed the stone to Charlie which took him a bit by surprise.

"I didn't want to wake you, so I went to fetch this. It's a book I used to read when I was younger. I think I used to copy all the pictures from it too but it's useless, there was nothing new in there that I didn't already know. Here you go page 28. It's got some stuff about rune stones on there. That's what it is, Charlie! Well that's what I think it is anyway." Tommy passed the book over to Charlie so that he could have a look. Tommy knew that Charlie was more academic than he was so he might be able to see something that he had missed.

"Oh, nice one, let's have a look then, oh! Tommy. You do know that this book is for kids, I don't think there is going to be loads of details."

Charlie took the history book from Tommy and started to scan his eyes over the pages in front of him.

"Here you go, mate, it's about as much as we are going to get from this book as far as matching the rune goes."

Charlie placed the book open on the end of Tommy's bed so that they both could see the page. He pointed to the picture at the bottom of the page. It was one of those hand drawn pictures that showed life at the time. There were a few huts scattered about and then some people in the foreground so you could see what they would have worn and some animals wandering around. However, Charlie's finger had rested on tall stones stood upright on the edge of the woodland.

When Charlie knew that Tommy was looking, he tapped his finger on the page. "That's our rune right there."

Sure enough, painted in the picture, carved as if it had been real, onto the side of one of the tall standing stones was the rune. Yes, there were some others, but they didn't recognise them. At the foot of the stone looked to be a man, dressed slightly differently to the others he was holding one arm up towards the sky and his head was tipped backwards, in his other hand he was holding a small leather bag and on the floor were several small stones.

"See here, Tommy, this guy here was like one of them witch doctor things, they could see stuff that was going to happen, and they used the runes to tell them, I think that's how it worked anyway. Here, you have a closer look, see if you can find anything else. I need to get off. I need to go and sort stuff out at home. Didn't leave on the best of terms with my mum last night."

"Yeah no problem."

Charlie wasn't really in the mood to be sitting here going through books. The evening's escapades had been great fun, but Charlie could not take his mind off sorting things out at home. He was feeling regretful about not going with his mum and it was just going to get worse the longer he left her. He stood up, grabbed his jumper and dragged it over his head. "Right, I'll leave you to it, can't put this off any longer, I'm going to get home."

"Do you not want any breakfast?"

"No, I'm good thanks, I'll get some toast or something when I get back, thought it might be good to get home before mum wakes up, maybe make her a cup of tea."

"Fair enough, sounds like a good plan, mate but we'll see you tonight and I'll tell you what I find out if anything."

Charlie left Tommy sitting in his room reading through the pages of the book and headed down the stairs. As he left, he pulled Tommy's front door shut behind him as quietly as he could so as not to wake Tommy's mum. He checked out the heavy clouds above his head, the rain was not pouring now but it was still coming down heavy enough to soak through his hair. He was taking a bit longer than he would normally on the walk back to his house because he knew he had to face his mum. He had not left on good terms and it would be an uncomfortable conversation that they were going to have when he arrived. It was only a short walk down through the centre of the village to his house and as he crossed the market place he glanced across at Zain's house and saw that his curtains were still closed.

Must be asleep, he thought. *Lucky thing, I'm shattered.*

Charlie reached his front door, placed the key in the lock and then hesitated. It didn't look like anybody was up yet so decided to go quietly. He turned the key and pushed the door open trying to keep the squeak as quiet as he could if that was in fact possible, the slower he went the louder it appeared to get. He stepped into the hallway and walked on through to the kitchen. As he went in, he saw his mum sat at the table.

"Hey, Mum," Charlie said hesitantly.

"Morning, Charlie, how are you?" Mrs Cooper was holding a cup of tea in her hands warming them. Charlie could see that she had not had a good night's sleep either and she was up earlier than usual.

"I'm good thanks, Mum, didn't sleep too well but..." He looked at her and didn't know if to say it for fear of the response. The room was silent, and his mum was just looking at him, so he knew he had to speak. "How are you, Mum, was it a good night?"

She tilted her head and gave a small smile. "It was good, thank you. Your sister had a great time, in all honesty she was happy that you didn't come but that doesn't mean that I didn't want you there. I did think about you while we were walking around, wondered where you were."

"I could see it, Mum, in fact you know with that lantern of yours I'm sure that I could pick you out from the crowd."

"Oh, Charlie don't be daft, I wish you would have come with us though. It's part of who we are as a family. Do you understand?"

"I get it now, Mum." He paused for a moment and looked up in to his mum's eyes and noticed that they had now started to fill with tears.

"In all honestly I think I would rather have been with you last night. We all talked about it and I'm definitely going next year." Charlie lifted his head and again looked at his mum's eyes, hoping that they were not now flowing with tears. She could tell by the look on his face that he was being genuine but didn't know why, not yet.

She reached over and put her arms around Charlie who hesitated slightly to respond in true teenage boy style.

"Are you too big for 'nuggles'?" The answer to which in her mind was always no despite how much he was going to protest.

"Nuggles, Mum? Seriously! Oh, go on then." Charlie also knew that he didn't really have a choice on the matter and to get on with it was the best way for all.

It was still a safe and warm feeling to be held by his mum, most teenagers wouldn't admit it but deep down it was the reassurance that most of them were actually calling out for and right now Charlie was happy for it. Charlie still knew that he had to make up with his mum for missing the procession and this was her reaching out and offering a branch. At the same time though he had to catch up with his friends tonight as he had so much to talk about. He went to pull away and then stopped. He had to sort this out with his mum first.

As much as he had enjoyed the chase of the night before it was playing on his mind. It had been scary and this was the first time he had experienced something like this, not that the others did this every weekend either, but it was, well out of his comfort zone.

"Mum, do you want a cup of tea?"

His mum just held her cup up and said, "Nice try, come on let's go and get on the sofa for a bit, we'll get the blankets out."

"Yep, nice idea, Mum, I might go and find some biscuits too. Never know when you are going to need a biscuit."

Charlie and his mum sat together on the sofa with the blankets wrapped around them. The TV was on but for Charlie it was just background noise. His thoughts had drifted off to the run through the park and the hedge that he should really think about going back to fix if he could. He then thought about when he had found the rune stone and the resulting chase. Oh dinner! He snapped out of his daydream suddenly.

"Mum, remember I'm off to Zain's this evening for dinner." He hated saying it as he knew it would hurt his mum, but he could work it.

"Yeah I know. Don't want to cancel and watch a film with your old mum, I'll make you popcorn? Yep, I'll let you have hot chocolate with marshmallows too."

"Oh, Mum that sounds good, but I need to sort, erm, sort some stuff out for a, erm history project that we are doing. Zain's mum and dad are expecting me too and they will have planned food and all that. Hey, I won't be too late though, Mum, what if I get back for nine o'clock? We could put a film on then. Would that be OK?"

His mum smiled and agreed.

"I suppose that's okay, but I get to choose the film."

"Alright, Mum, no romantic rubbish though please, oh, and please don't do the 'nuggles' thing in front of my friends, ever! They will absolutely rip me to shreds at school."

"Agreed."

Charlie slipped his trainers off, threw them into the corner of the room and sat back on the sofa. He reached over to the biscuit barrel, gestured towards his mum to make sure she didn't really want one and then grabbed a handful. "Mmm, chocolate cream biscuits the best!" Charlie could feel the warmth coming from the fire on the side of his face. Now this was a good place to be he thought.

Chapter Seven

Roast Potatoes (Saturday afternoon)

It was an unusual set up that the boys and their parents had come to, but it was one that was currently working and had done for some time now. Each weekend for most of the year the boys would have dinner on Saturday evening at each other's house. Zain's mum liked to have the company and she would fuss over them all afternoon. Tommy's mum and dad had taken the opportunity of the free time and would spend every third weekend, Saturdays that is, out and about which for them would mean a trip into Derby, clothes shopping, usually bringing Tommy a new top back.

Tommy's mum had not been happy to start with but when she realised that they could also go and spend a Saturday afternoon in the pub with their friends from the village like she used to do when she was younger at university, then she really took to the idea. A couple of hours out helped to relieve any stresses and it was always good to catch up on gossip around the village.

Mr and Mrs Talpur would always cook together, it was a great atmosphere when the boys came around to Zain's for Saturday night dinner. His parents would be in the kitchen each of them trying their hardest to make their special bit of the dinner better than the others but at the same time knowing that they had to make it work.

Charlie was stood on the porch having rung the doorbell. The smell of something fantastic cooking was filling the air around him as he waited for somebody to answer. He was just about to ring the bell again when the door opened.

"Hey, Charlie, come in. Head on through, dinner should be about an hour yet, we're running a bit behind today I'm afraid." Mr Talpur strolled off back through in to the kitchen potato and peeler in hands.

Today was no different to any other time they had gathered there. Charlie took off his shoes and placed them in the cupboard next to the door. He walked down the hallway and peeked in to the kitchen. Mr Talpur had returned to his duties and was now finely slicing what looked like cabbage.

Hmm, something different today, thought Charlie. However, he quickly dismissed the idea and looked back to see that Mrs Talpur was basting a chicken. Charlie knew there would be fine dining ahead of him and that was definitely good as far as he was concerned. He could have sworn that Zain had said curry but he loved a big roast dinner even more, especially when the weather turned in the autumn and winter. But first a few decisions had to be made with his friends.

As Charlie reached Zain's room, he could see that Tommy had already arrived and he and Zain were knelt down in front of Zain's bedroom window peering out across the marketplace.

"What's up, chaps?" asked Charlie, slightly confused by the positioning of his two friends.

"Ayup," Tommy and Zain replied simultaneously but had not turned their heads to greet their friend.

"I know that I'm going to get a really stupid answer from you so I'm not going to ask. Just budge up so I can see too."

Now all three boys were looking out of the window in silence, their arms resting just on the windowsill so that their heads were tucked away to peep over the edge. Charlie could not understand what they were looking at and could take it no longer. "What are we doing?"

"We're keeping watch to see if that BMW comes by again."

'Crich market place'

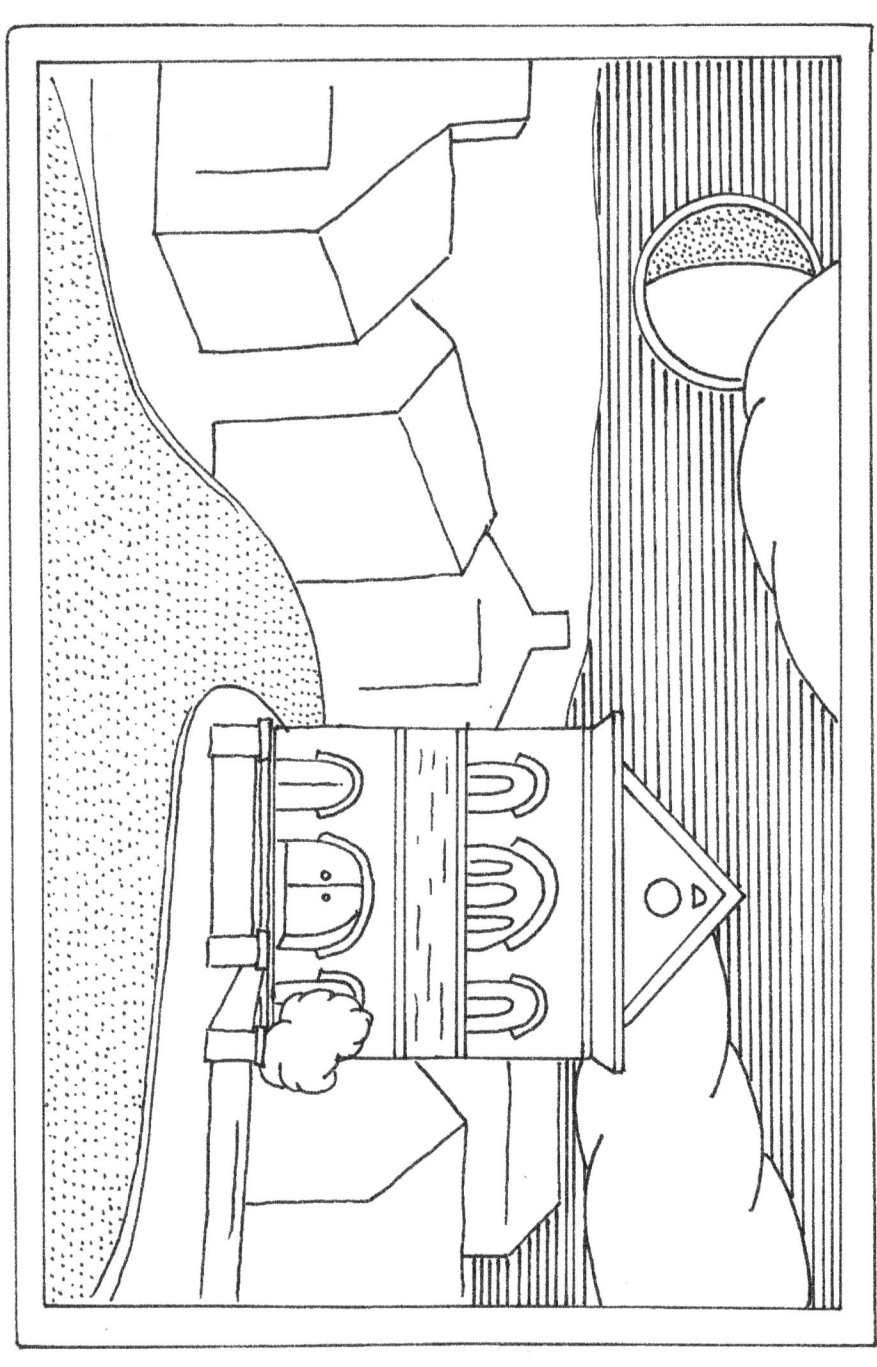

"Oh, man." Charlie was off. "How insane was last night? Those guys in that car chasing us was so..." He was unable to finish the sentence before the others joined in reflecting on what had gone on. They recounted their steps through the evening from meeting up to running back through the field down to Zain's house. They were finding it hard to believe that it had all really happened.

Tommy reached over and pulled his jacket off the back of the desk chair that was next to him. He placed his hand into the pocket and rummaged around for a moment. He then pulled out the rune stone and held it out for Zain and Charlie to see.

"Well we have this and that means that whatever happened last night was real and we are now a part of it."

"Dinner, lads," came a voice from downstairs. It was Mr Talpur and that meant there would be a table full of delicious food all laid out for them as soon as they could get there. The boys did not hang around and were up off the floor instantly filing out through the door and down the stairs.

"Yeah, now that's what I'm talking about, your dad is a fantastic cook, Zain, your mum too, I always enjoy coming here on Saturday. Roast potatoes, baby, yeah!"

"Nice to know you care, Tommy and I thought it was because you enjoyed the intellectual conversations." Mr Talpur had heard Tommy's comment as he was coming down the stairs. He was busy serving up the vegetables on to the plates set around the dinner table. At Zain's house it was more of a formal setting and they would eat with his parents. When it came to Saturdays at Tommy's and Charlie's it was more of a pizza and chips affair.

————————————

When the boys had finished, they still had duties to do. Surprisingly to Mr and Mrs Talpur the boys were up and washing pots, tidying everything away without having to be asked. It must have been a record time to have completely cleaned the kitchen and dining room. And then they were gone, straight back off upstairs.

"Thank you, Mr, Mrs Talpur, that was fantastic!" The words could be heard floating down the stairs as the boys ran off to talk about what to do with the rune stone.

They sat in Zain's bedroom all relaxing after a fantastic Sunday roast; it may have been Saturday but that's what they called it and that's what it was. The 'full works' as Mr Talpur kept reminding them.

"Look, lads we need to decide where we are going to keep the stone, I don't want to keep it in my coat pocket in case it falls out or what if I run into those blokes again and they catch me with it?" The others could hear the slight fear in Tommy's voice. "Besides, I've had it overnight and I've had proper weird dreams!"

"Leave it here then. I don't mind, after all, my house is kind of in the middle," replied Zain. "It should be safe here too; I can even lock it in the safe that Dad has down in the basement. I mean there's nothing else in it, I suppose that's why he gave me the code to it. Wait, hang on. I think I need to chat with my dad about how he only trusts me with things that aren't useful or worth anything anymore."

"Hang on," Tommy jumped in. "You're telling me that your own family doesn't trust you with things that are valuable or useful and you want us to leave you with what could be the most valuable thing any of us has ever had?"

Charlie knew that Tommy was only joking with Zain, he would trust him to look after a million pounds for him, if he had it, but he could still see the hurt in Zain's eyes, he might actually be feeling a bit let down by his parents. Charlie changed tack and tried to rebuild his friend's confidence a little. "Hey, you gonna show us this safe that you've got then?"

"Yeah, sure thing. It's in the basement."

The boys made their way out of Zain's room and on to the landing. Zain made sure his door was securely closed after him, as he didn't like his parents going in to his room, and then they made their way downstairs in to the hallway. Zain stopped next to the key hooks by the front door and sifted through. He picked several of them up until it looked like he was sure that he had found the correct one.

He made his way past Tommy and Charlie and placed the key into the lock on a small door that was underneath the staircase they had just come down.

"Do you know, Zain I must have been here a hundred times and I have honestly never noticed this door before."

"Well it blends in pretty well, I mean I hardly ever come down here personally, it's just Dad mainly, it's where he stores all of his stuff, junk from the house that we are getting rid of or stuff that he has collected and Mum hasn't allowed him to display it where anybody else can actually see it."

The door creaked as it opened and a draft of warm air came up from the basement bringing the fusty smell of damp old clothes. Zain reached around the corner of the wall without stepping onto the stairs that led downwards. His hand could be heard by the others as he fumbled around trying to find the light switch.

Zain turned around and looked at both of his friends, then he gave a short smile from the corner of his mouth and said, "I've been down there in the dark before and it's scary, alright."

They didn't need to argue with him just peering into the small doorway and seeing how the stairs curved around gave them a few goose bumps. The light flickered on and a warm yellow light cast shadows down the stairwell that made the basement seem almost darker than before; it still didn't look inviting.

The boys made their way down hesitantly. As they reached the bottom step, they could see that the room opened out in front of them and was larger than expected. It was amazing how much stuff you could fit into one room. All kinds of boxes of varying sizes were stacked up to the ceiling, paintings were stood up against each other, a clothes' horse stood full of who knew what, all covered in protective jackets to keep the dust off and there was even a token exercise bike that looked almost brand new.

Tommy placed his hand on the handlebars and looked at Zain raising his eyebrows and was ready to ask the question.

Zain got there first without even having to look at him. "It's my mum's, yes she does use it, no you can't have it and keep your feet off the pedals."

Zain went straight in and disappeared amongst the piles of boxes. The others could hear him rummaging around moving boxes from place to place. "Won't take long, lads it's over here somewhere, well it was last time I saw it. Dad comes in now and then and moves stuff around, I'll let you know when I get it. Oh and, Tommy. Stay off the bike!"

Tommy had put one of his feet on the pedals and then slowly removed it as quietly as he could.

"I never touched it, mate."

As Zain was busy and they knew that this could take some time given the amount of junk that was in the room, Charlie and Tommy started to take an interest in the boxes that stood either side of them and it wasn't long before they were pulling things out much to Zain's annoyance. As soon as they realised that, it was game on. It was like Aladin's cave, every box was packed to the brim and under every item was something more exciting than the last.

Charlie had found a load of old DVD's.

"Oh, man I haven't seen this since I was about nine years old. Oh, that's a blinding film." The running commentary continued.

Tommy was on his knees and was flicking paintings backwards and forwards. He lifted his head up slightly to see what Charlie was on about. As he caught sight of the title his head nodded in agreement. Then he went back to looking at the paintings.

When he looked back his hands had paused on a framed photo of Crich marketplace, it must have been old he thought. A group of men with all kinds of different top hats were posed in front of what was now the Indian restaurant.

"1895, I wonder what they did, well what were they doing. You know, it's strange looking at them standing there thinking that they once walked down what is pretty much the same road that you and I walk down today."

Charlie had moved on from the DVD's and had picked up a couple of cups and was now trying to read what was written on the side in the dim light that he had in the corner of the basement.

"Steady with those, Charlie, they're originals, in fact be careful with most of it please there's a lot of old stuff down here." Zain's voice came from behind a pile of boxes.

"What are they?" asked Charlie.

"Dad said they were here when we moved in, he found them down here in a small box all wrapped up in cloths. The cups were to commemorate Queen Victoria's Diamond Jubilee in 1897. I think he said that every child in the village was given one as part of a big party they had. That's where the procession started. The time of year has changed, I don't know why but they did a similar walk back then and had a big tea party in the marketplace. You must have read the plaque by the commemoration trees; you walk past it most days. Anyway, we do it up at the Tor now instead and I think the route is probably safer and easier if they don't have to shut off all of the roads and that sort of stuff."

Zain could see that he was going on and the others were now wanting to find the next item that took their interest. Charlie had already started to flick through a stack of old records that were on a shelf in the corner of the room and was quietly reading off the names of the bands.

"Beastie Boys hmm, Madonna, Whitney Houston, Prefab Sprout, never heard of them… oh, The Beatles!"

Tommy had returned to the paintings and was now actually looking at them in more detail. He was taking note of the type of frame that they were in, where they were set and if he could identify it, he liked the colours too, well lack of. The sepia tones gave him a feeling of nostalgia, even though he knew he wasn't from Crich originally it was home now, and he did have a feeling of pride. Derbyshire had been a good place to grow up in for sure, it wasn't as vibrant as living in Norwich itself, but he was kind of glad that he didn't have that city life anymore. He needed the space around him.

"Here we go."

Zain had finally found the safe, gathered the boys together and presented it to them.

"Seriously, Zain, you said a safe!" Charlie said shaking his head from side to side. "Well it'll do for now, Zain."

It wasn't much more than a tin sandwich box with a keypad for a code to be pressed in but thinking about it if they left it down here it could take some people a lifetime to find it if they didn't give up searching after the first five minutes.

Tommy stepped forward for a closer look. "No offence, mate but I think I could open that with a pair of plyers and a screwdriver if I wanted to. Possibly even a tin opener, you know one of those things you get in a Christmas cracker."

"Hey. I tell you what, Tommy, it's one hundred percent better than the safe you have."

"I don't have one," replied Tommy with a puzzled look on his face.

"Yeah exactly, hundred percent better, so let's agree then that this is where we keep it."

"Hey, it's fine by me. While you were messing around, I found this, here have a look. This, guys, looks to me like The Old Drinking Trough pub. Oh my word, you are not going to believe this." Tommy spun the picture back around and closer to his face to get a better look. "It's the rune! Look at the doorway above these two guys!"

The photograph showed part of Bowns Hill Road in the centre of the village. The Black Swan pub could be clearly seen and the barns that stand beside it too were also in shot. Somethings were different Tommy noticed like the fact that there were no paths and the road looked like it was just covered in gravel, he just loved the way the pictures faded off to the edges making it look like there was a mist surrounding the buildings. The main interest though was the barn to the left of the pub. On its side was a large sign, the wooden frame could be seen and the title 'The Old Drinking

Trough' was written arching over a large man holding a tankard with froth coming over the edge.

The doorway was open and in it stood two men facing in opposite directions as though they were not part of the photograph. Unless you had known to search, that is as much as you would have looked into it but because the boys had runes floating around their heads they were beginning to see them in all different places. The only thing this time is that it was actually there on the lintel above the doorway.

There were four runes marked across the top of the doorway, well they assumed that they were runes. It had been easy to identify the first as it was the same as the one on the rune stone that they now possessed. They were a little uncertain about the other shapes, as they were not like any letters from today's alphabet so they came to the conclusion that they too must be runes.

"Wait up! I knew that I had seen it before, but this isn't it. I mean this is bizarre, can it be that there are possibly two places in Crich that would have this shown? I'm telling you that there is another place in Crich that I have seen that rune before." Zain knew that he had seen the rune somewhere before, but he was wracking his brain to pull out the memory.

"It's the cross. The cross at the top of Bowns Hill."

"Well we've all seen that cross, but I don't remember there being any runes carved on it. Saying that, now I think about it I haven't actually looked at it that closely, y'know like when something is just there and it's familiar, but you don't pay attention to it."

"Well it's in the middle of the three roads so you are not likely to cross just to go and look at it and Charlie it's not on the front it's on the back."

Zain started to give a brief explanation to the others about how he had been shown the cross and then standing on it with his folks, had read the inscriptions. His dad had paid attention to the reverse side of the cross which was carved with a protractor and set of compasses with words about how the cross had been restored. Within this was the rune symbol as clear as day but out of sight. If you knew what you were looking for you would spot it a mile off but if not, it would just blend in.

"Do you think your dad might know? I mean he has all of this stuff down here in the basement and he must know what some of it means."

Charlie started to think about what Tommy had just said and he knew that Tommy had a point. It was true you wouldn't collect stuff without knowing something about it. With him being upstairs it would be daft not to go and ask him at the least. Tommy was already up the stairs and making his way out of the door.

"Back in a minute!"

Upstairs, Tommy had found Mr and Mrs Talpur sat in the living room. He poked his head around the door and gave a gentle cough to politely interrupt their TV viewing.

"Mr Talpur there was a picture downstairs, in the basement that I found, of the pub up the road 'The Old Drinking Trough'." Tommy knew Zain's dad's first name but thought he should always be respectful and do the formal thing by using his last name.

"Yep, I know the one, great little pub, been there for ages, good beer too but, well you'll have to wait just a bit longer. Won't be long I suppose until you guys are sat in there on a Saturday afternoon 'chilling out' with your school mates, well by then ex-school mates. What about it?"

"Well do you know anything about it especially the guys that are in the picture, is it anybody famous?"

"Oh, Tommy I don't know that much about the photographs I mainly collected them because it gave me a connection to the village. I have asked in there before and they told me that although it's not the same building there has been a hall of some sort in that area where they used to brew ale and mead, not sure if the chap in the picture is important though, might have been the landlord."

"Oh, OK thanks, Mr Talpur, you don't mind me having a look at them do you to see if there is anything else like that down there? I, erm, like to see what the village used to look like."

"Knock yourself out, Tommy, just be careful with them though. There are about twenty that I have that show different views some out over the fields as well if you like them too but they're all local."

"OK cheers," and with that Tommy was back off down the narrow stairs to report back to his friends.

Tommy came trundling back into the basement with a glum look on his face. "Well it was worth a try but he didn't really know any more than what we could have guessed, he just said that it's been there for some time and they have brewed beer there or near there for ages too."

"Look, guys I've got to get home, I said that I would watch a film with my mum. I say we meet up tomorrow morning and go and investigate both of them."

"Alright, mate, well I hope it goes well and yeah, knock on for me in the morning and we can go and check out the pub and the cross, OK?"

"You're on. Zain. Keep the rune safe," and with that the boys called it a night. Tommy thought that he would head off with Charlie and get home early too, better let his folks know that he was still around as he hadn't seen much of them in the last couple of days either.

Chapter Eight

A Second Sighting (Sunday)

Zain awoke to the sound of the church bells ringing, that meant that it had just gone 9:00. The bells woke him every Sunday, but it was comforting. Sunday was the day he liked to lay in bed, and this was the only day that his parents didn't bother him and would let him sleep in. Today was different though as he had agreed to meet with the boys at his house at 10:00. They now had a lead and they wanted to pursue it.

Zain opened his curtains and looked across the marketplace, which was still empty of cars, towards the Baptist Church. *What was that movement?* Out of the corner of his eye he had caught something move between the houses across the road. He kept watch for a few seconds unsure as to what he had just seen. He flung himself out of his bed and threw on a pair of jeans, put a jumper on over the t-shirt he had slept in and found a pair of socks that didn't have a hole in the toes. He was ready to go and find out more.

Before he headed downstairs Zain felt compelled to go back to his window. As he approached, the buildings came into view. The closer he got to the window the more he could see as they appeared to rise up from the ground. Was it there again, a shadow of a movement heading around the side of that house and through their garden gate?

That had to be a person, he thought, *but who is skulking around behind the houses and church?*

He waited again closely watching the spot where he thought he had seen something but there was nothing. They must have gone, or he was imagining it, so he made his way downstairs to grab some breakfast.

After a quick bite to eat Zain decided to wait by the window ready with anticipation, there was no need for his friends to knock on the door today. As soon as he saw Charlie coming across the marketplace he grabbed his coat and was off for the door. He called to his parents to let them know he was off out and slammed the door behind him. He was excited, imagine being the first to discover something this big going on in their little village. The thought of adventure was overwhelming him.

As the boys came closer to the pub, they could see the barn in question. The first thing they noticed was that the doorway was no longer there. This was not good news. Then as they drew closer it was also clear that the runes were no longer there either. They had been removed, by whom and why they did not know. All that was left was the chisel marks that crisscrossed over one another where once there had been carved runes.

They stood there for a few moments feeling deflated as they had lost what they thought was going to be a massive discovery.

Charlie was the first to speak, it was as though losing this made him want to find out more and fight on. "Lads, the symbols may have gone but don't you see what this means? Somebody thought that these were too important to leave here, they wanted to hide something. I don't think that we are the first people that have started to ask questions about these symbols, and they had to be protected." Tommy and Zain's heads began to nod in agreement.

Tommy reached out to the stone lintel and ran his hand over the wiped-out markings. "You're right, Charlie, if they didn't mean anything they would still be here. Zain you said that you had seen it on the cross, we should head up there and see if that is still there. If not, we know that they have been removed recently given that you saw it when you were younger."

"Well, well, morning, boys, you certainly do get around don't you, what's the adventure today?" Mr Pilcher had come from the courtyard at the side of the pub between the two buildings. To the best of the boys' knowledge there was no footpath down there, but hey, it was Mr Pilcher so it must have been okay for him to be down there.

"Morning, Mr Pilcher," the boys chorused. "Great day, Mr Pilcher," Charlie began. "We erm, we're just looking at the markings on this doorway and how they have been removed." He then chanced his luck, what with Mr Pilcher being knowledgeable about most things in the village. "You don't know who or why they were taken off do you?"

Mr Pilcher was caught slightly off guard as though he was not expecting to be questioned, not on that topic anyway.

"Well I... I believe that there did used to be some words there, but it must have had something to do with the pub, you know, advertising or something like that. I assume when it changed hands the new owners would have removed any old advertising or the old name."

"No! It wasn't a word, it was runes, you know like what the Vikings used." Charlie had been a little harsh with his reply, he knew that Mr Pilcher was covering.

Mr Pilcher's stature changed when he heard the word rune. He didn't respond for a short moment but instead started to case out the three boys. It was as if he was trying to assess how much they knew.

Tommy carried on from Charlie, "It was on an old photo of Crich that we found in his basement that's all, Mr Pilcher, not to worry, hey. We're off to the museum today to see if we can get some part-time work just at the weekends like, so we better get off. Enjoy the rest of your day."

With this the boys set off up the hill and past the school and the old Candlemaker's House. Tommy checked behind to see if Mr Picher had gone, he hadn't. He had remained at the pub standing on the pathway where they had had their brief conversation. He was standing with his left hand on the pub wall and was reaching up with his right to the lintel. As Tommy watched, Mr Pilcher moved his hands along the top of the doorway.

"Guys, he knows something." Tommy was concerned.

"I know, I mean I knew as soon as he started talking, lovely man but don't try and lie to a teenager. Keep walking though, Tommy we need him to think that we are just some kids playing about the village."

———————

A little farther along the road the boys were relieved to find that the stone cross was still there. Well they would have noticed that going, it was big enough to miss if somebody had moved it. Slap bang in the middle of the road junction you had to go past it or around it every time you came along this way. They crossed over the road and climbed up the three steps at the bottom of the cross.

"It's around this side," Zain directed his friends.

Zain moved around to the reverse side of the cross. "See there, there." He pointed to a carving at the top of the main shaft of the cross just below the circle. It was in relief and showed a set of compasses, a set square and a protractor overlaying one another with a shield and the words 'restored 1874'.

"That looks like my school maths set, Zain, but it's not the rune, mate. Maybe you just thought it, you know remembered it differently and changed it, what with all that has been happening."

"No, Tommy look harder at it." Zain stepped up closer and reached out with his hand. He placed his hand at the bottom left and slowly moved it. First upwards then diagonally to the top back down diagonally, he switched sides and carried on to the bottom right-hand side.

"See, it's been disguised, you know, hidden with these other objects. Whoever carved this, well renovated it in 1874, put the marker up, maybe that's when the other symbols were removed. It could have been the same person. A stonemason would have the tools and skills to do both jobs."

The boys looked in astonishment at what Zain had just shown them. There it was in plain sight as such. A hidden message but still a message to those who knew what to look for.

"I don't know what to suggest now, we've got two more clues that link this rune stone to our village." Tommy was also aware that they had been stood in the middle of the junction and soon people would be coming up to church. Mr Pilcher might even come up the road and if he was to see them well, he would be on to them.

Charlie's reply came and the seriousness could be heard. "I think that we should stay away from Pilcher for today and then at least until we want to speak with him, not the other way around. We could go over to St Mary's church. It's only up the road, it might be worth a little investigation. Might be nothing there but what if we could find evidence of a third symbol, it would make it concrete that we are on to something big. That church must have been around for a long time."

Zain had recalled his morning looking out through his window and seeing the movements. "It was Pilcher!"

"What was?" Charlie responded.

"This morning. I thought that I saw somebody across the road when I opened my curtains and then I thought I saw something a second time. It was him. I didn't see him, but I can feel it, guys, he's already watching us! He must be working with those guys in the BMW!"

This revelation had changed their mood. They had known Mr Pilcher a long time and trusted him, everybody in the village trusted him. To now think that he was up to something untoward did not bear thinking about.

"Now hang on, Zain, this guy is like the model villager and everybody respects him. Do you really think that he has done all of that, to now be sneaking around the village early in the morning hiding when he thinks that somebody might see him? It's a bit far-fetched, mate."

Zain wasn't convinced but he didn't want to push it with his friend.

———————————

As the boys now had nothing better to do and no other suggestion had come out, it made sense to go and look at the church too. They set off on the short walk to the churchyard and agreed that they could have a look around, ten or fifteen minutes before the parishioners arrived for service. A quick check on the church building itself and then to look through the gravestones to see if anything matched.

St Mary's church was positioned towards the top end of the village. It had originally been built in 1135 but like so many other small village churches, as the village grew more space was needed so it had several extensions so to speak over the centuries. The entrance to the churchyard was covered by an ornate timber archway, the gate to which was always open. As soon as you entered the gravestones started to fill in from either side which were interspersed by mature Yew trees.

The boys split up and started to scout around. They tried to get in as close as they could to the original structure and had wanted to go in but by the sounds of it there were people inside as the morning service must have started. Tommy was taking a close look at the large double oak doors as Charlie was checking around the inside of the porch.

"There aren't any scratch marks on that door are there?" Charlie asked as he quickly looked at the door.

"No, why?" replied Tommy slightly confused as he didn't really understand what Charlie was asking him to check.

"Just making sure The Shuck hasn't been calling, c'mon there's nothing in here let's go and find Zain in the yard."

Tommy followed Charlie, still with a puzzled expression on his face, around the side of the church and found Zain who had been going around what he thought looked like the oldest gravestones and tombs. He was carefully stepping around one of the larger tombs at the far end of the graveyard when the others reached him.

"We couldn't see anything around this side. Let's just check these few, have a glance around the back and then call it a day, I'm starting to get a bit hungry."

The boys slowly moved from stone to stone casting their eyes over them to see if they could find anything.

"Charlie." There was a short pause. "Charlie, I don't want to worry you."

"What is it, Zain?"

"I don't think that we are alone anymore!"

The boys stood still as an ominous feeling fell over them. Charlie gave a shudder as a cold streak ran down his body. Tommy had started to twitch his fingers together, something he did when he was nervous. He didn't think that the others knew about it but they had seen him do it whenever he talked to girls that he liked and put two and two together. Zain was getting pretty good now at spotting when things were not quite right, so it was becoming standard practice to listen to him.

The churchyard was noticeably quiet, and it was only now that they thought about it there was also a lack of birds whistling. It was too quiet, if that could be a real thing.

"Hide!" Charlie spoke out just in time.

This sense of Zain's had saved them a second time for around the edge of the church porch came two men dressed in dark blue overalls and t-shirts. They were down to earth clothes and well, not smart enough thought the boys for somebody who has heading for a service at the church but neither did it look like they were the sort of people who come out to do a bit of grave rubbing for a hobby.

"It's the men from the black BMW. I know it is, just know it is, they've come back to get us!" Zain whispered to his two friends. He had not actually seen the men as he had been the first to dive down behind the tomb.

Tommy took it upon himself to check so had crept towards the edge of the tomb that they had found to hide behind and peeked around the corner. "No, I don't recognise them, but I reckon that it's the Burrowdale blokes!"

The boys were now sat with their backs against one of the tombs that were dotted around the graveyard, next to which was a large Yew tree that thankfully for them had not been pruned for a long time. The lower branches gave them the additional cover they needed to remain hidden from the threat that approached them.

They huddled in together pulling their heads down out of sight. They could hear the two men walking down the path, pausing now and then, but they were, however, drawing closer. It was only a matter of time before they would pass the edge of the tomb and stumble across the boys sat there. Tommy was on the end and had spotted a low point in the wall where it had partly been damaged over the previous winter. A few layers of the stone were now missing but it was enough for them to be able to vault over. They would then be in the cemetery car park and be able to get out into the fields or down and around the back of the houses.

'Bong, ding, dong', the sound of the bells filled the air around them, this marked the end of the service and just in time. There was a shuffle of feet on the end of the gravel path next to where they were sitting, and the footsteps went back up the path towards the church door. Tommy chanced a peek around the edge of the tomb.

"They're going, let's go now while we can!"

The boys were up on their heels as quick as a flash and were heading directly for the gap in the wall. As they clambered over Charlie turned around to make sure that the men had gone only to spot them standing by the archway at the entrance to the churchyard. They were staring directly at the boys. For a moment both parties stood their ground and then the Burrowdale men slowly walked forwards. It was surreal to watch them advancing slowly through the crowd of people who were now filing out from the church. They looked polite and respectful as they were saying morning to the people as they passed by, but the boys knew their intention.

There was no need to hang around any longer it was only a matter of moments before the Burrowdale men would be able to start to chase after them without causing any suspicion. The boys turned and fled. Across the car park and through the gap in the hedge at the end of the lane. This path took them back around the outside of the village. After a few hundred metres they turned right in to the woodland that ran along the side of the path. They knew it was private property but Tommy who was out in front had a route home in mind and they were not about to stop to debate the morals of nipping through somebody else's woods. They came out between two houses about two hundred metres down from the church entrance. They quickly looked up and down the road. Nothing. Across they went and down the road until they reached the path that would take them through to the park.

They were clear.

As they hit the park Charlie chanced a look at the hedge that he had fallen into on Friday night.

Must fix that, he thought.

Zain had been running with his keys in his hands and had been fumbling with them to get to the correct one for the garden gate. Tommy and Charlie were hard on his heels and could see the gateway to his garden. It was after all the closest of their three houses, so it had made sense to get there and hide out.

"Oh c'mon, c'mon, why do you all look the same?" said Zain as the keys continued to slip through his fingers.

"Bit racist, mate, we're running as fast as we can," Tommy replied.

"Not now, Tommy! I'm trying to get the key, are they behind us?"

Tommy could tell that Zain was getting stressed so spun around and checked across the park to where the path came in from the road. "No, it's clear, we're good to go, get the gate open as quick as you can."

Zain had finally found the correct key to open the Yale lock and he held it out in front of him as he moved across the final few metres. He hit the gate, the key went straight in, and he shouldered his way through. The guys followed and with one last check to see if anybody was chasing, they closed the gate behind them.

The boys fell back against the gate and fence. Everything went silent and all they could hear was the sound of their hearts beating in their ears and their heavy breathing as they recovered from one of the quickest eight hundred metres they had ever run. If only their sports teacher could have seen them, he would have been really impressed, they probably would have made the athletics' team.

"This is getting all screwed up, we have got to tell somebody!" Zain was panicking.

"Wow! Hold on, Zain, just calm it down, you're safe, okay, you're safe, they're not going to do anything even if they ever caught up with us."

Tommy knew what Zain meant but he had to try and help him chill out a bit first, it was getting a bit out of hand to have people chasing them around, but the thrill was overtaking him and he didn't want it to stop. Involving their parents now would mean handing the rune over to them and probably ending the whole adventure. It would go to the museum or be taken away and locked up so that it could not be seen again. Tommy was not going to let that happen if he could.

———————

Back inside the house the boys began to relax slightly. However, Zain had clearly been affected by the second chase of the weekend.

"There are now two or three lots of people on the lookout for us. This is some seriously screwed up stuff over a little stone." Zain was still thinking about who might find him and possibly what they might do to him if he was not able to give them the answers they wanted.

"Zain, I've just had a thought. Do you mind if I go and get that photograph from downstairs? You know, the one we were looking at yesterday of the pub." Tommy's face had lit up as if he had just experienced something for the first time.

"No not at all, rather you than me, I don't want to go down there right now, just make sure you switch the light off when you come back up, yeah."

Tommy had only been gone a few moments when he came panting back into the room. He placed the photograph down in front of his friends and asked them to look at it again. The picture looked different today, it was still the same street and buildings but because they were now part of what was happening it had become familiar and comfortable. Charlie and Zain held the picture closer and started to examine it but could not yet see what Tommy was getting at.

Tommy took the photo from Charlie's hand and turned it around to face them. "Well, you two may not have had a good look but I feel that I was close enough to smell the guy's breakfast on his breath. This guy here in the photo is the spitting image of our new friends the Burrowdales, well one of 'em anyway."

"No way!" Charlie paused and looked at the man again. "You have got to be kidding me, that can't be right." He took a second look at the image and tried to get the picture as close to his face as he could to see the details. He was in no doubt either, there was no hiding that face. "They must be related they have to be to look that similar."

Zain was taking everything in that was being said and had started to formulate an idea. "Now if he looks the same as him and that symbol is the same as the one we have on our stone, that's up on the main road and we all know about the stones, it can only mean one thing don't you agree?"

Tommy was on him. "Zain, I agree, that I don't think I have ever heard a worse sentence in my life. Strangely though I know what you mean." He looked him in the eye and said it out straight. "Yes, mate I agree!"

"These Burrowdale men know what's happening!"

"This rune stone, Tommy, there is something important about it and these guys, well they've known that for a long time! The stories must have been passed on to them from their parents, grandparents, we don't know how long it's been going on."

"Then it leads to something. In some way this stone can, I don't know, it can show you the way, or it tells you something. We know that the symbol, rune, is an old sort of language but even so it needs to be in some sort of context for us to understand what it is telling us."

This revelation brought it home to the boys and now they started to understand that they were now part of something that had been going on for a long time. There were secrets here and there were people out there that were trying to keep it that way. They were not sure right now who they could trust to talk to about the rune stone but they knew that they had to find out more.

That evening Charlie had done his duty and had supported his mum in cooking the dinner and then washing up. He thought it a bit unfair that his sister was able to get away with not helping but his mum would always tell him that he never helped at her age and when she was older, she would be doing the jobs too. He had decided to get an early night, after all, it was school in the morning and he was feeling everything catch up with him, physically and emotionally.

Charlie lay in his bed. He was rolling the hot water bottle over between his feet trying to get them warm without burning them. Sunday was supposed to be a day of rest, thought Charlie and he was happy that he was resting now but his feelings about the weekend had changed. He would rather have a month of these types of Sundays than just sitting around. The more he thought about it the more excited he became with the thought of adventure. He began to mull over everything that he and the others knew about the rune stone and how it fit in with the village. The photograph was at least a hundred years old and the stone even more. The Merryweather Stone, the standing stones, well they had been there for at least a thousand years.

But they had hit a wall and they could not go any further or learn any more about the rune with what they currently knew. He pondered on how he could get information, the library in Matlock would have some resources they could use and they might be able to get something from the museum in Derby. He was sure that when he went there when he was younger there had been some Viking stuff. This is when it came to him. He had thought of the perfect person to ask. He would be like a font of knowledge. Any question they ask he would be obliged to answer, after all, that was his job. Charlie was now cobbling together an idea of how to get his history teacher to tell them everything they wanted to know without letting him know that they were up to something.

He had to get his plan together tonight, they had the class tomorrow afternoon and they needed to know as much as they could. The questions started to pour into his head, and he was visualising his classroom and how they would all be sat: where Alison would be sat, what Tommy would need to ask, how to get the rune checked, what he would say to Alison when he saw her next.

Charlie was drifting off and his thoughts changed, he was now out in the hills walking with his friends, the sun was hot and shining in his eyes, but he knew that the sky was a beautiful bright blue. He could imagine the warm breeze blowing on his face, and the leaves on the trees around them were rustling. He couldn't hear what his friends were saying but he could see them smiling and their laughter was clear to him, Alison was laughing. His eyes blinked slowly closed, open, closed one more time and then he fell into a deep sleep.

Chapter Nine

A Bus Stop Chat (Monday)

Zain sat at the breakfast bar looking at his toast with distaste. He would rather have had a bowl of chocolate cereal but his parents had found out that he had been spending all of his lunch money on sweets instead of what they called 'proper food' so they had banned all chocolate in the house. He could hear some of his other school mates starting to pass the front of his house on their way to the bus stop just outside his house, but he hadn't seen Tommy or Charlie yet. The view from his kitchen window allowed him to look across part of the village square. He glanced at the clock: 7:50am, he still had at least another fifteen minutes before the bus arrived that would take him to school.

Zain's mum passed by the doorway behind him and called through, "Make sure you finish your breakfast please, Zain."

"Yep, will do," he replied and bit a piece of toast off to show goodwill. It was definitely not the way he liked to start his day and he wished it was the weekend again.

His thoughts drifted off to all that had happened and wondered how the day would go. He so wanted to talk to somebody about the events of the last few days but had agreed with the others to keep it quiet until they knew what they were dealing with.

There was a sharp knock at the door, Zain jumped up threw the last of his toast in the bin and placed his plate next to the sink.

"Off to school, Mum," he called. "See you later when I get home." He grabbed his coat and his keys from the rack and went out of the door.

Tommy and Charlie stood either side of the porchway waiting for Zain but mainly to keep out of the rain. Tommy was in his black hoodie, wet patches clearly showing on each of his shoulders. Charlie being slightly wiser had decided to put his coat on, however, it hadn't stopped his hair getting wet which had now started to fall over his forehead and every now and then a drop of water would fall.

"Well?" said Tommy looking at Zain inquisitively.

"No, I didn't," Zain paused and thought it would be funny to then end his sentence, "enjoy my toast."

"You know what we mean."

"Yeah, I know, I just like winding you up. I haven't mentioned it to anybody, OK!"

"Good. Now I've had a proper good thought about history class this afternoon. C'mon, better head down to the bus stop."

The boys walked slowly down the path towards the bus stop and said hello to a few of their school mates who had started to gather. The three of them closed in together and looking around to make sure that nobody was listening Charlie started to explain his ideas for that afternoon's lesson.

Charlie enjoyed the history classes that he had so far this year. Mr Reynolds was new to the school and had taken on teaching the year 9 groups. Charlie thought that Mr Reynolds made the topics interesting to learn about. He told loads of stories but would throw in all of the dates and figures and names of people and events that they needed to know about, but he had also noticed that if you started to ask questions as long as you asked the right way, you could easily take him off track. Many of the lessons had taken this course as the others in the room had asked silly questions. They were usually about a tv show that they were watching and wanted to know if it was historically correct.

Charlie had the window seat and had placed his bag on the seat next to him. Friends in groups of three meant that one of you would be sat by yourself and today was his day. He didn't want some year 7 muppet sat next to him, bringing his credibility down. Charlie turned to look out of the window, but the glass had all steamed up. He reached into his bag and found a tissue that he had left over from a couple of weeks ago when he had a cold. Wiping the window Charlie's attention was caught by the blue phone box at the Tramway museum. He had seen it a thousand times before but today was different. He recalled when he was sat there with Tommy and Zain, it felt like a different life, could it really have only been forty-eight hours ago?

He drifted off and started to recall an episode of Dr Who that he had watched last year or was it the year before? His eyes flicked back to life and he started to watch the trees go by through the window. He loved the colours of the trees in autumn, and as they dropped down out of the moors, they became more plentiful. The hills definitely came alive with beautiful oranges, reds and yellows. The rain clouds came down and clung to the tops of the hills across the valley, small wisps reaching outwards like fingers grasping out to stroke the trees as they drifted by.

The bus started to drop down the hill through Holloway towards Lea Bridge and the John Smedley mill. He looked around and saw that the others on the bus were continuing with their conversations in their usual groups. He could see Alison sat towards the front of the bus. She appeared to be happy chatting with her friend. He so wanted to know how she was but knew that time had passed. After all, he now had a new mission. He needed to know about this rune stone. Charlie watched the river gently flowing by, slightly higher than normal, he thought.

One last pick up in Cromford where around another ten kids would get on and then it would be another five minutes up to the school in Matlock. It was strange for Charlie to feel nervous before school. Sure he had felt nervous on his first day, when there had been a test or he had to give a presentation to the rest of his group, everybody had felt like that, but today he could feel the butterflies in his belly. For the first time in a long while Charlie felt that school was really important and that he needed to get the most out of the day as he could. He finally understood it.

The bus pulled up in the layby outside of the school and the rest of the passengers all rushed and pushed to get off. The boys waited their turn patiently remaining in their seats until the bus had cleared. They climbed down from the bus and paused at the school gates. With the rain still falling quite heavily most of the other students had gone straight inside, there were just a few stragglers hanging on before their lessons started.

It wasn't the most modern of buildings, but Charlie liked his school. It was large enough for him to not feel like he was being watched all of the time but at the same time small enough to know pretty much everybody who was there. Considering that the students came from all of the local villages to come here he knew that if he went to any of the surrounding areas, he would be guaranteed to know somebody there.

"C'mon, let's get this done, I've got geography first," said Tommy, "so I'll see you at break."

And with that they strolled through the front doors towards their respective lessons.

Tommy had spent the majority of his geography lesson drawing a little map of Crich in the back of his book. He had started to piece all of the information together on to this diagram. He had drawn on where the stones were and where they could place the rune images. He wanted to see if there was a pattern to them. After a few minutes of this he had turned to drawing doodles of cars including the BMW that had followed them on Friday.

Charlie had geography too but had been placed in a different group to Tommy, in fact this was the only time that they did not have a class together. He had other friends in there, but it was weird not having his best mates in with him. This is where Charlie had first really met with Emma. Due to his teacher sitting them boy/girl, boy/girl he had been placed with her. He had known who she was before they sat together but over the first year, they had become quite good friends not outside of class but they both appeared to enjoy sitting with each other. This class had gone quickly as it always did. Charlie was enthusiastic when it came to this topic and he was well versed with what his teachers were telling him so he could relax in the class and enjoy it. The fact that he and Emma also had a joke made it a great way to start the week.

Zain meanwhile had chosen to do one of the vocational options and was, at the moment, doing cooking. This had been the best session that he had done in his mind. He guessed that he was taking after or had got this from his dad's passion in the kitchen. It had been a little basic for him today because his dad had shown him how to do this years ago, but he was busy making a sausage plait. The fact that it was easy allowed his thoughts to wander off. He was thinking of the Burrowdale men and Mr Pilcher and the two guys in the black car. He was also wondering how they could possibly all know about the rune stone and how long this had all been going on for. Were they the second people to come into its possession or had there been many more like them before?

Zain refocused onto his class work. He had been plaiting without concentrating and when he looked down at his work it was there. As he had folded the strips of pastry over one another he had done it in such a manner as to fold the rune into his pastry. He gazed at it unsure what was happening. He checked around the room to ensure that nobody had seen and slowly unfolded the pastry.

Chapter Ten

A Lesson in History (Monday)

Lunch time had arrived and not too soon for Tommy and Charlie. They found geography OK but at this stage in the year they were starting to prepare for their exams and the revision exercises were starting to become tiresome, one question blending into the next.

Zain was already sat in the dining hall tucking into his packed lunch. Charlie had spotted him and started to make his way over whilst Tommy went off to join the queue. Chips, cheese and curry sauce was his normal lunch. It sounded nauseating to most people, but Charlie had tried it once and he had to admit it was pretty tasty.

"Charlie, I need to talk to you while Tommy isn't here."

Charlie checked over his shoulder and could see that Tommy was chatting to another girl from their year, he didn't stand a chance, but it would keep him occupied for five minutes.

"What's up?"

"It's this rune it gets in your head! I've been seeing it everywhere. That's not weird is it, Charlie?"

Charlie looked at his friend's face trying to get a sense of what he was truly thinking beyond the slight fear that was in his eyes.

"I tell you what, Zain, since the day we found it, I've thought about nothing else. Both nights it's been in my dreams somehow, do you understand? It's not just you!"

"Yeah, yeah, I understand, Charlie. Hey, we need to confirm what we are going to do this afternoon."

Charlie and Zain had been discussing the plan for the history lesson and hadn't noticed Tommy sitting down.

"Oh man, these are good today," Tommy blurted, blowing out at the same time as the last chip was slightly too hot to chew.

The distinct and delightful smell of salt and vinegar on chips wafted across Charlie's nostrils distracting him. He snapped out of it and looked at Tommy then carried on. "We're all set for this afternoon, I'll start off by getting him going and then you guys step in with a couple of questions, he'll be hooked. That'll also keep him from thinking that it's just me trying to derail his class."

———————————

Charlie had the best seat in the classroom for history, well that's what most of the others thought, he was near the back of the classroom next to the window and he shared a table with Emma again. Nearly everybody Charlie knew had asked him at some point to put a word in for them. 'C'mon, Charlie, you sit with her, just get her to come out on Friday so I can meet her, y'know'. Well that was the normal request.

The lesson had started in its normal way, everybody was sat in their usual place and there was a distinct look of disinterest on the students' faces as they thought about the hour ahead of them filled with dates and names of people they had never heard of. Mr Reynolds sat at the front of the class preparing to take the register. Before Mr Reynolds could start, Charlie thought it best to get his question in. "Sir, I know we did about the Vikings in year 8 but do you know much about them?"

Mr Reynolds looked up from his desk and scanned the room until he found the student that had voiced the question. "Yes, Charlie of course I know about them, they did play quite a big part in the history of the country."

Tommy stepped in quickly. "Sir, were 'They' ever in Derbyshire, sir because Charlie said that I look like a Viking the other day?" This wasn't true but Tommy was trying to keep his teacher on track. If he could get a teacher to defend a student from being called something that wasn't true that was their first goal achieved.

"Well, Tommy without stereotyping you don't have a typical Viking look so to speak but yes, Tommy of course they came into Derbyshire, well it was called Mercia then one of the Saxon kingdoms." He strolled over to a map that was posted to the wall next to the whiteboard and had pointed to roughly where Crich was on it. He swept his hand around and Charlie knew that they were in.

"So, where did they first come into England, sir?" Tommy carried on with the questions.

Mr Reynolds continued to talk about the first sightings that had been documented and how the locals had been slayed. He moved on to the next area of England, as it is now, and started to talk about Norfolk. Tommy was distracted as this was where he had been born. Charlie had to get his teacher back on track, he couldn't let him just ramble on.

"So, sir whereabouts did they live around here then?"

Mr Reynolds paused for a moment. They could see him thinking, it was like he was flicking through pages of a book only one that was in his head as his eyes had started to roll over and then flick side to side. "Well, Charlie, first we have to understand that Crich may have been called 'Cruc' back then, a name dating back possibly to the Roman times. We could probably place Danes in this area around Monyash. What's that, about ten miles away from here? I mean there is nothing concrete to say but it is believed there was some sort of settlement for a while anyway."

Zain saw his opportunity and started to ask his first question. "Sir. If the Vikings wrote their words in runes how do we know what they were saying?"

This was truly fantastic for Mr Reynolds, the happiness had come back in to his eyes as he thought that the students who were sat in front of him were starting to take on what he had been teaching them and now had their own genuine interest in his subjects. "Well, Zain, there are many examples of runes around. The runes themselves are said to have come from the Well of Urd. In the lore of the god Odin or Woden, we hear how he hung from 'Yggdrasil' or the World Tree in order for him to understand the meaning of the runes. You see, Odin knew that they had meaning and if he could understand them, he would be wiser. He could also see that runes had more than just a meaning and from all of this the Viking or Norse also believed that they had magical powers."

Mr Reynolds was on form; show a little bit of interest and he would talk all afternoon. He was starting to gabble at a good pace now as he recalled the information and the boys were trying to understand all of what was being said to them whilst picking out the important parts that they really wanted to know. It was funny to see and maybe Zain had been wrong, but Tommy was actually taking notes into the back of his book rather than drawing doodles.

Mr Reynolds continued, "Different versions have existed over the years and it also depended on the region, for example the earliest form is now known as 'Elder Futhark' and it's about 1500 years old." He turned and faced the window and walked closer to look out across the fields towards the hills. "And then there is the later version 'Younger Futhark'."

Mr Reynolds moved across the room with a moment of inspiration. He was busy drawing on the board and was giving examples of runes. This was it, what they really needed if they were to understand the stone that they had.

Zain stood up from his chair, he had never done this before in a classroom. He could sense that the others in the room had all turned their focus to him apart from Mr Reynolds who was still busy on the whiteboard. He paused as the fear rolled over him, and he was compelled to sit down again. His stomach churned and his head spun. He rubbed his thumbs across his fingertips and the sweat was unbelievable. He looked around for support and could see Charlie waving him on and mouthing the words, 'Go, go do it now'. Zain composed himself for a couple of seconds and found the courage and carried on. He cautiously walked towards the whiteboard at the front of the classroom where Mr Reynolds had been frantically drawing the examples of the runes that he knew, calling out words, names and meanings.

As Zain approached, he spoke out, "Could I borrow the pen please, sir, it's just that I've seen a rune before and I wondered if you could tell us what it means if I drew it on the board?"

Mr Reynolds was slightly taken aback as he had not noticed Zain walking up behind him. "Er, of course you can, and I will if I can, tell you what it means."

Zain took the whiteboard pen from his teacher's hand as he passed it to him. Zain gave his teacher a nervous smirk in return. Mr Reynolds' face was covered with puzzlement as he watched this student who had never really taken part in the lessons before now, stand at the front of his class and start to draw a shape on the board. Zain was steadily drawing the rune from the stone and was trying to add the three-dimensional aspects.

"Hmm let me see there. Now I am not a specialist you understand that don't you, but I do recognise it, this is called 'Othala'. The meaning of it though I would have to look up if you wanted to go that far."

Zain had to think quickly as he could see that he was about to be sent away. He tried to recall the other shapes that he had seen on the photograph from his basement.

"Is there one that looks like this, sir?" He roughly sketched out a second symbol that looked like a letter 'M'.

"Well it looks like a rune as I recall them, but I think you have got me on this one, Zain. Look, what I will do is a bit of research and bring a few more examples in for you all if that's what you would like?"

"Yeah that would be great, sir if you would." Zain reluctantly handed the pen back to his teacher, but he could not think of how else to get anything further from him. He walked back towards his chair as he looked around for his two friends for support and to see if they were happy with what he had achieved.

Charlie had been busy watching Zain at the front of the class, impressed with his mate's performance and had not noticed that Emma was leaning over and talking to Alison who was sat on the next desk. He could not believe this was happening, what were they saying? Were they talking about him? He could feel that his hands had gone sweaty and he had lost all focus on what they had set out to do. Zain had started to fluster too at the front of the class. He could sort of hear his bumbling 'yes sir, that's nice, lovely, oh man what is he doing', but he couldn't help him as the girls had taken his attention.

Before he knew it, Emma and Alison had both turned and looked at him. He froze and smiled with what must have been the most gormless look anybody had ever seen. They both chuckled and went back to their little huddle.

"Oh fantastic," the words came out silently. He could feel his face starting to burn up with embarrassment as he noticed Zain shuffle past him towards the back row. He looked up to find Tommy staring straight at him nodding his head. Tommy then stuck both thumbs up at him. Charlie felt even more awkward and wanted the class to end.

———————

Mr Reynolds had started to notice that some of his group had begun to drift off and become disengaged and duly reverted to getting them back on task. "Today then if you could turn to…" There was a slight groan from Charlie's classmates as they realised that they now had to actually do some work.

Thankfully for Charlie the rest of the session went quickly without anything else to worry him. He had kept his head down and just got on with the task that he had been set and could not wait to catch up with his friends at break.

As the bell rang Mr Reynolds was still talking. The whole class grabbed their bags and coats and started to make their way out of the room. There were a few 'thank you, sir' which the boys had not heard for a long time coming out of a history session. Emma had packed her pens and books away and had stood up and turned to face him blocking his way. "See you later, Charlie. You guys have made it fun today thanks." Emma leant inwards towards Charlie. "Oh yeah, and she still likes you. You just need to talk to her, okay?"

Charlie could feel the smile start to form on his face. "Cheers, Emma. Oh we, didn't do it on purpose we were, er, just asking questions, you know how it is." It wasn't his most convincing performance, but he had to try to get Emma to believe him.

"Yeah OK. We'll talk about it another time. Anyway, see you later." Emma turned and went on her way leaving Charlie sat at his desk.

Tommy and Zain had packed their stuff away and were making their way over to Charlie who was still smiling. They were looking at him wondering what Emma had just said to him to make him smile.

"Well, boys, I guess I've still got it, apparently Alison still likes me. So, thanks for all your advice and confidence in me maybe I'll go and see her after school later."

"Never mind that, we've got things to talk about, what with everything we have learnt today, that was great." Tommy was chuffed with what they had found out and wanted to get down to fitting it all together.

———————

School was over for another day and the boys sat on the school bus near the middle for their homeward journey. They had tried for the back where they could get more privacy but were too late. It was difficult to talk without being overheard so waited until they arrived back in Crich.

The boys had taken in all that their teacher had told them in class, Charlie thought how good it was that Tommy had actually paid attention which must have been a first for him in a long time. Charlie considered how Mr Reynolds must have thought he was doing the best lesson in the world having engaged Tommy in the discussion. What they had learnt was helping them to piece together how and why the stone would be in Derbyshire and it would also explain the standing stones.

"I can't come out tonight, guys, I've got my aunty coming over and we haven't seen her since last Christmas so Mum said that given that I didn't go with her on Friday night I should at least be there tonight. She has been laying it on pretty thick, every time I see her, she just gives me one of those looks, you know, there's no way of winning even if I be nice and do what she asks, it's just not good enough. I know I went and watched the film with her, but I still have a long way to go. I blame you two really for making me come out on Friday."

"Hey, hey, hey, we did not make you come out, well Zain did but I didn't." Tommy's timing was perfect and just enough to catch Zain out.

"Oh, you git! I didn't ask him to come out, you did!"

"Look, anyway, lads, whilst you two decide who to blame for getting me to come out on Friday I'd better get going, I'll see you in the morning."

Charlie checked out who was still in the marketplace from his other school friends and could not see anybody. He pulled his bag up higher on to his shoulder and headed off down the road while Tommy and Zain continued to chat. He had now started to think about how his mum would be when she got home from work and how the evening would go. He needed to make sure he was back in her good books and had even thought about making a start on preparing dinner for everybody. With all this Charlie soon reached his front door and made his way in.

"A cup of tea might be good and maybe a little treat from the cupboard just to keep you going, eh, Charlie?" Charlie was chuntering to himself as he went down the hallway and into the kitchen.

———————

Before Charlie had reached the cupboard, there came a sudden bang on his front door startling him, which he thought was bizarre behaviour as he had literally just closed it behind him. Why would anybody do that?

"Let us in quick." The muffled calls for help from his friends could be heard through the door. A rapid banging came again this time from two sets of hands.

Charlie opened the door and no sooner had he turned the latch than his friends came rolling in through the doorway bowling him over. Tommy and Zain stumbled on Charlie who was now on the floor in his hallway and it was only a moment before they were all piled up on top of each other. Zain, having been the last one through the door was currently lying on top and was able to spin his leg around in order to give the door a quick tap knocking it closed.

"They're back, the guys in the BMW. We had to come here, or they would have seen us, and we can't let them know where we live."

"Oh, I see, so it's okay to let them know where I live, you gits."

"No, it's not that. They would have seen Zain going into his house and I would have had to go past them." Tommy gave his blunt reasoning which Charlie kind of accepted.

Charlie pushed Tommy off and pulled himself to his feet. Then he went to the door and looked through the peep hole. "Well that is absolutely useless, anything more than a metre away looks blurred and upside down, it could be Santa stood outside and I wouldn't recognise him!"

"When you are ready to get off me feel free!" Tommy started and then Zain realised that he was still lying on top of him.

"We can go into the spare room upstairs. We should be able to get a good view down the road to see where they are." Charlie started to scramble up the stairs and the others followed. He ran through into the spare room at the front of the house and pulled the curtains together so that there was only a small gap left for him to look through.

"What can you see, tell us what you can see?" called Zain.

"Alright, Zain, chill out man, let me look." Charlie placed his head through the gap in the curtains and scoured the street in front of him for the black BMW they had seen the other night.

"Are they there? They were parked just around the corner on Sandy Lane. They must have been watching the school bus." Zain edged up to the side of Charlie and pulled the curtain back slightly to point in the direction of where he and Tommy had seen the car moments earlier.

"I know where Sandy Lane is, Zain. Well it's nowhere to be seen now so they must have, wait, get back!" Charlie pulled away from the window into the darkness of the room. The curtains fell back inwards towards each other and swayed gently.

"What was it did you see it?" Zain was visibly showing signs of being excited by the chase, knowing that he was safe in the house.

Charlie could still see the road from where he was stood and paused as he watched the car drive by. He could see that the driver was clearly focused on the road ahead which made him feel better as it meant that they had not seen Tommy and Zain or if they had they didn't know who they were. He could also tell though that he was not a happy man.

"It's them alright. The same driver, well from what I could see anyway. This rune stone is worth something and they want it back. Do you know if it was a wallet that we had found or a watch or something like that I would have taken it in to the police station, you know, handed it in, but it's the way that these guys are behaving that makes me not trust them. I don't believe that they got the rune stone honestly and I don't believe they have good intentions for it whatever it is that 'It' does."

Tommy stood next to Charlie and was nodding his head. "I'm with you on that one. They don't seem right. We need to be careful though because I don't think they would take kindly to finding out that it was with us." Tommy stepped forward a little and with his hand at arm's-length drew the curtain back slightly for a better view.

"Charlie, it was bright under the street lights that night when we ran into them, there is a good chance that they will recognise us eventually especially if they see all three of us together, y'know, it'll jog their memories or it will look familiar to them and who knows what will happen then." Zain was always good for building their confidence in a situation.

"Zain, it's going to be OK." Charlie was trying to be as reassuring as he could, although he too knew the consequences.

Chapter Eleven

Where to Next? (Tuesday)

Tuesday had come and gone at school and the journey home had also been uneventful. Most of the day the boys were apart due to their differing classes and during breaks it was difficult to discuss the rune stone with all the other students going around them. They had finally sat together on the way home and decided to go to Charlie's when they got off the bus in Crich. Zain's house was closer but his mum would be home so she would start to hover around if they all came back and then she would want to find out what they were doing.

Charlie opened his front door and the boys stepped in calmly this time to his relief. Charlie knew that his mum would be at work until five and his sister was at the childminder's so they had about an hour of time before they would be back. They were finally free to talk without having to look at who was around them. They went into the dining room at the front of the house. Charlie walked over to the small bay window and drew the curtains partially together. After having the car drive by yesterday, he was feeling a little exposed sitting in view of the window.

Tommy had been building up to this all day and had to get everything off his chest as quickly as he could so started to rant. "Look it doesn't make sense. I didn't know until yesterday that the Vikings were ever supposed to have been in this part of England, I mean it's like York, everybody knows they were there but Crich! I didn't think there was anything here to show that they were here. So how did all this stuff get here?"

"Well, that's a good question, Tommy. Look, the thing is that this stuff is here, we just never thought to look for it before and at some point in time the Vikings must have been here, and that stone proves it. It's got to be for something, it's too good, y'know fancy, for just a normal rune stone so I think that it's something unique." Charlie was speaking slower than he usually would to calm Tommy down. "I think the fact that the runes appeared on the side of the pub and up at the cross says something different though. We know that they don't date back to the Viking times so somebody else put them there which means that they must have known about the rune stone."

"It's a good point, Charlie, we really have stumbled upon something and I don't think those people had taken into account three teenagers who were just hanging around to have found their stone."

"No but I don't think that it will take them long to start to ask questions and if we are not careful, I mean if we tell our friends, that it will lead them back to us."

Tommy had stopped listening to Charlie momentarily as he had spotted the edge of a photo sticking out from one of Charlie's schoolbooks on the bookshelf and could not resist annoying his friend for a bit of light relief. "See you've dug that out. Why do you still have a photo of Alison hanging around? I thought when you 'split up' we agreed the best thing to do was to get rid of all those photos and bits you had?"

Alison was never supposed to go out with Charlie because she was too good for him, that's what most people had said around the school, but it happened. They had been together for about six months and then it all fell apart. Charlie had never really understood why but he knew that a lot of other people at school were getting involved and were making it difficult for them. What he did know was that the news from Emma had made him feel good and he wanted to hear it from Alison herself.

"Do you mind, Tommy, perhaps you could take a little less interest in my love life and think about the situation that we are in? We need to be a bit more serious given that those blokes yesterday did not look best pleased when they came past. I know it was dark the other night, but I could see them, and I have no doubt that they could see us. They've seen our faces that means that it's only a matter of time before they find one of us. You are right though, not about Ali, but sometimes just because something in history isn't recorded it doesn't mean that it didn't happen. There are loads of cases where things have been omitted from records or even removed on purpose just so that it or they were forgotten. In this case though…" Charlie paused and started to speculate on what could really be happening.

Zain had been sat listening to his friends but had an idea of his own and at this point decided to share it. "Yeah, so I was watching a documentary about the Egyptians and they had defaced whole temples just to remove the carvings of one of the Pharoahs so that they would be forgotten. To me though it's like one of those stories where they have hidden a treasure and only certain people know the clues to look for and without them it will be hidden forever."

"Well there's something that we could research another day. We could try and find out if there are any stories in history for this area of a treasure going missing? It might be worth a shot. I never thought that I would say this but at the weekend we could head into Derby and check out the museum?"

"Derby, yeah I'm in, I need to get a new top." They had lost Tommy who was now starting to think about a new jumper. A good thing in some ways, as he had worn this one solidly for what must be well over six weeks and a change was due. It was getting close to five o'clock and Charlie's mum would be home soon, so the boys packed up and decided to head on home.

The boys left Charlie's house and walked back towards the marketplace. Charlie had been given instructions to get a loaf of bread so thought he should make sure that he got it before his mum got home. He could also walk his mates part of the way back up the road.

When they reached the baker's, the boys went their separate ways and agreed the time to meet up at Zain's later. Charlie was unsure of his feelings, there was an aspect of excitement and adventure, but the anxiety was niggling at him as he wasn't wholly sure if he could take another evening of events like that of Friday.

Charlie stepped into the baker's shop and headed over to the shelves to select the bread. He was stood deciding which type of loaf to buy and was debating with himself; he liked the Bloomers but his mum really liked the Tiger bread. He knew that he had been stood there for some time and that it was just bread at the end of the day, but this was important, and he had to get it right for his mum. He heard the bell on the shop door ring behind him. He paid it no attention and continued to debate the two different types of loaves in front of him. A strange sensation came over him, he could feel the presence of somebody stood behind him. Fight or flight was the first thought to fly through his mind.

"Hi." The voice was soft and familiar. He felt his heart beat faster. It was a voice that Charlie had wanted to hear for a long time but had not known how to get her to speak to him. This was his chance to make it work. Alison was here in the shop and she had come over to him. This was the first time that they had spoken in three months.

Charlie was having a number of thoughts about how to respond then realised that he had not, and it was starting to look like he was ignoring her. He had to think fast but the more he thought the harder it was to decide what to say. 'C'mon, Charlie, speak you fool' and then it happened.

He turned around to face her. "Oh, hey, just buying bread." 'Just buying bread! Just buying bread!' What a muppet! Charlie knew that was one of the most stupid things that he could have said being stood in a baker's, but he had to go with it now. He tried again before Alison could speak.

"How are you?" He looked up and into her eyes. It had felt like such a long time since he looked at her. He started to recall all the elements of her face that he had liked. Her hair had fallen slightly over the edge of her left eye as it always used to do. They looked a darker brown than he remembered but still large like 'Minstrels', as he had once said.

"I'm good thank you, Charlie. I'm just buying a loaf of bread." She tilted her head to one side and gave him a smile, mocking him.

Charlie's heart had started to race, his hands were sweating, it was like being together for the first time all over again.

"Well, madame, I could recommend a lovely Tiger bread, or we also have here some beautiful cobs in this corner, but it really does depend on what you were planning on having with your bread." He gave a smile in return and then turned more serious. "I've been wanting to speak to you for ages but it, well, I think you know what I mean, well I hope you do? I don't really know how to explain it." Charlie could see on Alison's face that she was in agreement and hadn't appreciated how everybody else had gotten involved with 'their' relationship which had caused it to end and she too had wanted to see him.

"I understand, Charlie."

"Alison, you know I would like to stay here and chat but I've got to get home, I need to be making a good impression with Mum and this is one of those things she has asked me to do so I need to make sure I get it right. I'd really like to see you again if you want to? Maybe we could meet up at the weekend?"

"Yeah. I'd like that, Charlie. Look, don't tell anybody though, not yet. I just don't want all the talking to start up again. I want us to have some time for us and not be the thing to talk about around school. Is that okay?"

"Is that okay! That's absolutely perfect by me. I'll call you later in the week when I know what I am up to at the weekend. It's been. It's been really good to see you."

Alison reached out and touched Charlie's hand. "It's been good to see you too. Make sure you call me." With that Alison went out of the shop and Charlie took his Tiger bread to the counter.

Hey, she didn't even buy any bread? and at that point he was smitten. Once again.

Chapter Twelve

Return to the Tor (Tuesday Night)

G iven the events of the last few days the boys had decided on a more discreet and out of sight route to the Tor. They knew they had to get back there but didn't want any unexpected guests in order to give them time for a proper look around. 8:00pm, Tommy and Charlie were in the pre-arranged rendezvous, crouched in the front garden of Zain's house. He appeared from the side gate keeping out of sight from the road as he crouched down next to them.

"Okay, just picked up a torch in case we need one," said Zain.

The sun had long set and the evening was really starting to turn cool. The boys had planned a route that would keep them out of sight from any prying eyes and most of all where they could be away from the roads so that if there was anybody driving around looking for them, they would not be found. They stepped across the driveway and pushed through a small gap in the hedge in to next door's front garden. They bent down and crawled under the two front windows of the house and climbed over the low wall into the small area at the corner of the marketplace, where a bench had been placed for visitors to rest.

This was it. They checked around to see if anybody was taking an interest in their activities. 8:15pm on a Tuesday in Crich, there would be nobody around, but the boys thought it prudent to check. The village was quiet, as usual, with the odd car passing them by as they waited behind the wall to make their move. Tommy was first to speak. "Look, we can't stay here all night we have to go because if someone sees us it is going to look really dodgy."

"Oh yeah and my mum is not happy that I'm out again tonight, last thing I need is for somebody to tell her I was crawling around in people's gardens."

"Well go home if you want to. Zain and I can go and have a look," replied Tommy.

"Not a chance, it's far too much fun. Beats sitting on that rock for another evening."

At that point Mrs Crow the old lady from down Charlie's road crossed over the street and made her way into the shop. The coast was now clear, they knew this was a good time to go. Across the road and between the houses then over the hedge, that was the plan, but they ended up crawling through the hedge which was slightly larger than any of them remembered. It was also slightly more painful than any of them had hoped because it turned out to be a Hawthorn bush.

"Nice plan, lads, why didn't we think to have a quick look down here when it was light and then we would have known that there was a giant hedge in the way?" said Tommy.

"Well then somebody could have seen us, and they might have wondered what we were up to, you know how it works." Charlie was right as usual.

"It never used to be that tall," Zain mumbled feeling slightly judged by the others as they rubbed at small scratches on their hands and faces. It had been his suggestion to come this way after all.

Once in the field behind the houses and the boys knew that they had not been followed, a sense of relief came over them. They got their heads together and forged on with their mission. Tommy was actually having fun if not taking it a little too seriously. He had started to use hand signals to communicate which was a great idea if only the others could have understood the meaning of wiggly fingers and waving hands and, if they had cared for his little role-playing. It was clear that they were by themselves and speaking softly was enough precaution needed for the present.

"Stop messing about, Tommy," said Charlie.

"Thought it would add an element of mystery and excitement," replied Tommy, slightly deflated by his companions' lack of engagement in the role-playing.

The boys reached their second obstacle, the road to South Wingfield, which cut down and across the hill in front of them. It was a matter of finding another gap in the hedge, but luckily when they did find one it was opposite an opening on the other side of the road where the farmer must have gone in and out of the fields. A quick check to make sure it was clear, and they were on their way again.

They went past the farm and through the fields around the edge of the village, until they reached the back of St Mary's churchyard and the memories of Sunday started to fill their minds. Each of them was conscious of where they were and were looking into and around the graveyard, at any moment expecting to see the Burrowdale men.

After half an hour of skirting around the village the boys had reached the far side of the Tor. This was far enough, any farther would have brought them too close to the old quarry edge. They walked through the edge of the woodland, following the limestone gravel path until the trees parted revealing the Memorial Tower standing tall, high on the summit of the hill in front of them. The village now lay way down the hill on their left, quiet and still, the street lights starting to flicker as the rain advanced in their direction.

This vantage point was perfect as they could see anybody approaching in front of them from at least three hundred metres away, plenty of time to hide or run and nobody in their right mind would trudge through the mud field like they had just done. The cliff guarded their right-hand side.

Zain had once again been on lookout at the front of the group, and every now and then he stepped up on to his tiptoes in order to see a little farther along the path which made him look a bit like a Meerkat. "Hey, we're all clear, guys, there is nobody and I mean nobody up here."

The wind had picked up as the night had gone on which had really made the temperature drop. The top of the hill being exposed the way it was meant that the wind was blowing straight up against the boys and they were now beginning to feel it. The odd spot of rain was now adding to the chill.

"I can't stay up here too long, Charlie it's blooming freezing!"

"I know, Zain but we are here now and while there is nobody else here, we should take advantage of it and see what we can find, if anything!"

Zain knew that Charlie was right in that it would have been a wasted journey to have come so far and then gone straight home again.

The boys made their way to the spot where they had first seen the two men standing, as they presumed they must have known something about where to look. They started to scour the Memorial Tower for any signs of markings that resembled the rune stone. Tommy was now pushing stones in the hope of finding a secret compartment. The next step was to search around the door, there might be a carving like on the cross in town but again there was nothing.

"This is fruitless, Charlie we haven't found a thing, I mean nothing, not even a sign of a marking, there must be something we are missing." Tommy would have stayed longer if Charlie and Zain had wanted them to, but it wouldn't have been much longer as his fingers were now going numb.

"C'mon, it's too cold, let's get back."

Tommy and Zain were glad that Charlie had spoken out, being up here tonight in the cold was grim and having found nothing of interest it was taking its toll on their spirits. The decision was made quickly to head to Zain's to review their little outing.

———————

The boys had reached Zain's house and were now sat down around the kitchen table. Tommy was busy putting the code back into the keypad lock in order to keep the rune stone safe and Charlie was reaching over the back of his chair to try and warm his hands next to the radiator.

Zain had been rummaging around the cupboards quietly and had finally found the biscuit tin that had been moved again in order to stop him from eating every last morsel and he placed it on the table in front of the others, which brought a smile to all of their faces. He then moved on to stirring the three cups of tea which the boys now desperately needed, firstly to help get warm, but also to raise their moods. It was clear on their faces that they were disappointed by their evening and lack of anything new to help them. Zain placed the tea on the table spinning the cup handles around to face his guests, his attention was now on food.

Zain opened the biscuit tin. "Oh man, Digestives, Rich Tea! This is some kind of sick joke, my parents are twisted, why would you buy these when there are so many other great biscuits out there, with crème and chocolate. I could go a Bourbon right now, you get where I'm coming from?"

Zain had gone to his special place and until his cravings were resolved he would be on about this for days, 'biscuit gate'. Charlie had taken note of Zain's plight and was knowingly searching in his jacket pocket. There came a gentle rustle of a plastic bag. Zain's eyes opened wider, his lips curled up at either side of his mouth and the tiniest of contented smiles came across his face.

"Here you go, mate you can have these. Wait." He paused for a second. "I think you deserve them." Charlie had pulled a small packet of chocolate coated animal shaped biscuits from his pocket that he had left over from school earlier.

"Yes, man, now that is what I am talking about, in your face Mum and Dad, chocolate for the Zainster."

"Zainster? That doesn't work. Please don't do that in public especially if I am around. I will give you biscuits everyday if you promise." Charlie was serious, he had a reputation to maintain, so he thought, and he wanted to keep it the way it was.

The mood in the group had changed for the positive having thawed out and had a cup of tea, however, they all now felt that they were almost at an end to their adventure with no more clues to follow. Running around the streets and being chased had been exciting but reading books and researching to find out information was not their idea of fun and having to do that in order to take the next step was not looking good for them, not to mention how long it would take them.

———————————

It was starting to get late and the boys still had school in the morning. Charlie and Tommy said their goodnights to Zain and made their way out of the door. Zain returned to the kitchen to tidy up before going to bed. It felt empty without his friends and looking around he noticed that the safety box had been left out on the table. Tommy was supposed to have put it away, under the stairs, but he must have been distracted by the tea and biscuits.

Zain went to pick up the safety box ready to take it back in to the basement but instead he sat down at the table again. He could not resist the temptation of having a closer look at the stone so opened the lock. When he looked inside, for a moment he thought that it had gone. The stone was so dark in its colour that it appeared not to be there. He panicked for that split second before his eyes adjusted to the darkness. With relief, Zain took the stone out and held it up to the light above the kitchen table. He studied the carving until his fascination drew him to look closer at the rock itself.

"What am I doing sitting studying a rock, this is ridiculous."

Zain placed the stone down on the table just in front of him. He then rested his elbows onto the table edge, lowered his head on to his hands and started to contemplate the situation he had now found himself in. He was feeling the tiredness come over him and was beginning to find it difficult to keep his eyes open. As he drifted in and out of sleep, he thought that he could hear the strangest of noises coming from the table below his head. It was as if something was being dragged slowly across the table. For a moment he did not move with fear and then he slowly tilted his head to look at the table.

Startled with what was happening in front of him he rubbed his eyes as he could not quite believe what he was seeing. He looked more intently, his eyes focusing clearly on the rune stone.

It is, it is, he thought. There was a faint tap of stone on metal.

"Well I didn't expect you to do that! Oh, and now I'm talking to a stone and to myself too!"

Zain had just witnessed the stone moving albeit slowly, but it had still moved. The stone had turned in a clockwise direction and had only stopped when it had hit the biscuit tin. He had to check or at least to see if it would do it again. For a moment he doubted it and considered the level of the table running his hand over the table to see if it was level and then trying to wobble it. No, it was the stone that moved.

He placed the rune stone into the middle of the table and sat back. He wasn't sure how long he had watched waiting but nothing had happened. He couldn't see what was different and then it came to him. He placed his hand on the biscuit tin and slid it slowly across the table towards the stone.

"You moved! Ha!" Zain cried this to the stone directly as though he had beaten it at its own game. "That's two to the Zainster!"

He pulled the tin away and carried out the experiment again. Movement. He tried it again at different distances and even placed the tin on the other side of the stone. At the right distance there was motion from the rune stone, always in a clockwise direction he had noticed, but why that direction he couldn't work out. He knew that this was the next clue and it was this discovery that would enable the boys to move on. The only problem he had now was that he would have to wait until the morning to tell his friends his exciting discovery.

Zain opened the drawer that was underneath the table top and rummaged around until he found the piece of fabric that he had been looking for. He picked up the rune stone and carefully wrapped it up within the cloth in order to protect it.

"There, that's better, you'll be safer inside this but maybe I need to find a bag for you tomorrow, a proper bag, a nice little leather bag maybe."

Zain placed the rune stone inside the small safety box and took it back underneath the stairs. He was happy that the rune stone was away and would be protected for the evening. He made his way off to bed and could not wait to see his friends in the morning in order to tell them what he had discovered.

Chapter Thirteen

"You Want a Clue, I'll Give You a Clue." (Wednesday)

Zain had woken early with excitement and had hardly touched his breakfast, toast again. Obviously, he had pretended every time that his mum was nearby but all he wanted to do now was to see his friends. He had already been under the stairs and collected 'his' rune stone and was sat at the table eagerly looking through the window for his friends approaching. He held the rune stone close to his chest, gently in his cupped hands being careful to make sure that when his mum went by, she could not see.

Charlie was the first around the corner and Zain was up on his feet in a flash running towards the door. He opened it pre-emptively, caught his friend's attention and beckoned him over. As Charlie reached the edge of the marketplace Tommy came bounding down the road. They both reached Zain's front door at the same time.

"Morning, gentlemen," called Tommy.

Zain could not hold it in any longer so did not even respond to Tommy's greeting.

"You wanted the next clue well I've found it and you are not going to believe this, come in and sit!"

Zain was how they would say 'buzzing'. Charlie and Tommy loved to see him like this but could not work out what he was so happy about. Zain had already opened the safe and was giving the rune stone a little polish on his t-shirt before he placed it in the middle of the table in front of them.

"Yes, Zain we've seen it before. Oh, and did you just clean it?" asked Tommy with confusion.

"Er? Yeah, just looking after it you know. Anyway sit."

Zain had purposefully placed the rune with the carved side facing upwards, it acted like an arrow that was currently facing Tommy. Zain looked at both of his friends and gave a little chuckle but did not say anything to them. He reached over for the biscuit tin and placed it on the table just at the right distance that he had worked out last night to enable the stone to rotate.

"Oh no thanks, mate I've just had my breakfast," Tommy said, which had taken Charlie's eye off the stone.

Charlie looked back down at the table and then on to the stone. His left eyebrow raised slightly as he realised that something was different. His eyes lifted and looked at Zain, who was already aware that Charlie had worked it out.

"How did you do that? How did you make it move?"

Tommy was now even more confused with the situation and wanted to know what was happening.

"It wasn't me. It's the stone itself, I think it's magnetic. I mean it's attracted to the biscuit tin. It only goes clockwise but it has a reaction whenever it is in proximity to the tin."

The stone sat in the middle of the kitchen table. The boys were sat on either side of the table staring. The room must have been quiet for a good five minutes as they all took on board what they had just witnessed. The silence was only broken by the entrance of Zain's dog Darwin who had decided to barge his way through the kitchen door slamming it against the wall as he began to investigate what was happening and why all of these people were now sat in 'his' kitchen.

"That's not a clue, Zain, that's epic!" Tommy was brilliant sometimes with his level of enthusiasm.

Charlie needed to clear the matter in his own mind and spoke up.

"This is important. I mean it's special; discovery of the century, it's unique and it's here with us. We need to decide what to do. So, we either take it back to the Tor and throw it aside for those guys to find, pretend it never existed, or we take it to Mr Reynolds, hand it over and see if he knows what to do with it and it will probably end up in a museum. Or and I mean or, we look for more clues and see if we can find out why all this is going on here."

Charlie did not know truly how much the others wanted to be involved. To him it was the most exciting thing that had happened, possibly ever, but he wanted it to be all three of them. He looked both of his friends in the eye and hoped he knew them as well as he thought he did.

Zain's lip curled upwards in one corner as he began to speak. "I'm in, man, why let others have the fun? Scared the hell out of me being chased by those blokes and the thought of running in to them at any point, but what a rush."

Tommy knew he didn't have to give an answer either way, Charlie knew he would have gone with him, but he felt it was needed. "Let's do it."

The boys had gone on to chat about all the adventures they were expecting with most of the conversation consisting of 'imagine if…' and 'wouldn't it be great if…' and 'then this would happen…' It was only when Zain mentioned treasure that it started to become real.

"You don't really think there might be some sort of hoard of treasure here in the fields somewhere?" Tommy asked.

"Well you never know, there was that guy in Kent who found a chest of Roman coins and that mask, shield thing they found in Norfolk."

"Look we've put the clues together and we have some good ideas, but we don't know where to go next, it could be ages before we discover anything else."

Zain and Tommy knew that Charlie was right on his last point, the Tor had come up empty and the photo had set them off but also ended up nowhere except with more questions. Mr Reynolds had given them loads of useful information, but it didn't show them where to go.

"Hey, it's five to eight we need to get going or we'll miss the bus."

Zain snatched the rune from the table and placed it carefully back into the safe. He closed the front and spun the lock, then gave it a quick rattle and shake to make sure that it was locked. He had found that the box would fit nicely on the shelf just inside and above the basement door so no longer needed to head all the way down the stairs. Pulling the door closed he was ready to head off to catch the bus with the others.

———————————

Mrs Cooper stood outside the local shop as she watched the school bus pulling away and just caught a glimpse of Charlie sat looking out from the window and hoped that he would have a good day.

"Right, pick up the milk and then off to work. Oh."

As she turned around, she nearly fell straight over Mr Pilcher. She had not heard him approaching and wasn't sure if he had come from inside the shop or down the alleyway at the side. One thing she did know that he wasn't there when she had walked down the street.

"Morning, Sally, beautiful day?" He did ask but it wasn't really the question he was wanting to know the answer to. Mr Pilcher continued before she could answer.

"I saw your boy out on Friday night with two of his mates, up to mischief I bet, I definitely was at their age. I didn't see him at the procession though, was he busy?"

Sally thought it a bit strange as Mr Pilcher had never taken this much interest in Charlie before. Sure, he had said hello, but this was different. Even so, she felt compelled to answer him trying not to offend him. "Well you know how it is when they start growing up, it's far too uncool to be seen out with your old mum especially when your friends are not going to be there either. He's been busy with a history project that the three of them are doing."

"History, hey, well if it's about Crich send them my way and I might be able to give them some information. It must be about the buildings here in the village. Oh, you see they were asking me about The Old Drinking Trough on Sunday too."

Sally looked at Mr Pilcher and was finding it difficult to understand where he was going with his conversation.

"Mr Pilcher that's ever so kind of you and I'm sure that the boys might come and ask you some questions if they get stuck, I'll be sure to pass the message on. If you would excuse me though I need to just do a few bits in the shop before my bus arrives."

"Of course not, Sally. You have a good day at work now." Mr Pilcher gave a smile that made her feel uncomfortable.

Sally made her way into the shop and as she closed the door, she took a quick look to see where Mr Pilcher had gone. He was slowly walking across the marketplace towards the Methodist Church and then disappeared around the corner of the building.

Chapter Fourteen

'Are You for Real, Zain?' (Thursday)

Having spent most of their day deliberating what action to take next the boys had finally decided it was time to go back to the beginning. There they stood all in a line staring across the field from the Sitting Stone. The three sticks they had been using to play 'Flicky' were still laying at the side of the path where they had dropped them.

There was a gentle breeze blowing up over the field, which was slightly warmer than the last few days, however, the clouds were still hanging heavy in the sky, dark grey and full of rain, waiting to soak them one more time. The boys knew that at any moment it was going to start. The mood was different somehow. Now as they looked around the place it was no longer enough, this was not a bad thing, they wanted to move on, reach out and see more. They had outgrown the Sitting Stone, something had changed within them. One thing was for sure, they were definitely more confident. This was their village and strangers would not come in and spoil it.

Over the day the boys had formulated the plan. Zain had put the pieces of the puzzle together during his English class. The idea was now to bring the rune stone and Merryweather Stone together. The boys presumed this is how far the men in the BMW had gotten and that's what had led them to the Memorial tower. They just needed to confirm it all.

"Nobody about, Tommy, Charlie, did you hear me? I said nobody about. Now is the time to do this." Zain had made the call to move, he wanted to check over the Merryweather Stone in the remaining daylight. They approached the Merryweather Stone from the field, this time they would not be caught out by anybody and should anybody come they would be able to duck down behind the wall between them and the road. They could see the top of the Merryweather Stone on the other side of the lane and made their way up to the wall.

"Tommy keep an eye out down the road and give us enough warning to get hidden should we need to. I think Zain deserves to place the rune on the stone, without his discovery we would not have made it to this point."

"Sounds fair enough. Oi! Zain, don't break it!" Tommy was happy to let Zain take this moment of glory but thought it only right to give him some grief first.

Zain had taken care of the rune stone since they had decided to keep it at his house. He reached into his inside coat pocket and pulled out the stone. He had now taken the step of wrapping it in a cloth that he had found, the others had noticed, so it took on a ceremonious air as he unwrapped the stone. He folded the cloth carefully back up and placed it inside his pocket.

"Zain, I know I said you deserved to do this but if you take any longer I'm gonna rip that stone from your hands, chap and do it myself. Walk over there, place it on the rock, watch it for a bit and then tell us everything that it is doing. Remember people are on the look-out for us and if that was me this would be one of those places I'd be looking. So, do you think it would be possible if we could get on with this at some point today?"

Zain was standing silently with the rune stone in his open hand. He calmly took a deep breath and blew out then gave his remark back to Charlie. "Could have done it by now if you hadn't done the speech, just sayin' like."

"Zain! You're stressing me out!" squeaked Charlie.

"Yeah I know."

Zain approached the Merryweather Stone and rubbed his left hand over the top of the standing stone. He could clearly feel an indentation that would house the rune. He brought the rune closer and placed it into the shallow dip. His hand hovered over the stone for a short moment and then he let it go and watched.

The reaction was instantaneous. Zain could not believe his eyes, from seeing the reaction in his kitchen it was now happening for real here out in a field. This standing stone had been placed here a thousand years ago, roughly, and it was still working. This was the concept that got to his head the most. But it was working and the rune stone was gently rotating, clockwise. Charlie had been observing from the middle of the road but had moved closer as he could not resist seeing what was happening. He caught the end of the rune's motion and with it his jaw had dropped.

"Tommy, it's working, man, it's working. Zain where has it stopped?"

Zain took a moment to respond, he was still overwhelmed that it had worked. "It's, erm, it's pointing that way." He raised his arm and pointed directly across the village and at the Memorial Tower.

"Car!" Tommy called out loud and clear.

The call of approaching danger had startled both Charlie and Zain. Zain almost jumped backwards and nearly fell over the small wall that he had been stood next to. Even though it was a call out for danger Tommy couldn't help but chuckle. The sight of Charlie skipping back and forward on the spot, in the middle of the road, his brain processing, trying to work out what to do, run for cover or head back to grab his friend, amused him. It was only when Zain righted himself and picked up the rune stone that Charlie knew he could go.

There at the far end of the lane a car had just turned in and was currently stationary, its headlights facing in their direction. As the boys knew this road was seldom used that meant trouble. After their little moment, Zain and Charlie were across the road in a shot and back into the field. The plan had been to hide behind the nearest wall, but it looked as though Tommy had a better idea. Either that or he had forgotten the plan as he was already halfway up the hill. Tommy and Zain didn't hold back and were soon close behind him. A few more metres and they would be at the gorse bushes from which they would be able to observe and be suitably hidden.

As they got into position the car sure enough pulled up at the spot where they had all just been stood. It was the same car, the black BMW. The decision to run had been a good one but Charlie thought that he had better praise Tommy later as for now he had to watch and see what would unfold.

"Well this takes me back, it's just like the good old days."

"Good old days what are you on about?" Charlie was confused by what Tommy was saying. He was tucked in behind the gorse, but his mind was still running checks on what was going on around him making sure that he was safe.

"Well Friday night, we were sat here weren't we looking down at that car. Okay, it was facing the other way and I know that can be confusing to some people. But you know, the good old days."

"Thank you, Tommy! Are they still in the car?"

Tommy had positioned himself well being the first to get there so that meant that he had the best view. He could see the car clearly but while it sat there, there was no sign of any motion outside. A torch beam shone from the driver's side of the car and moved about, slowly lighting up the area around the Merryweather Stone and along the ground around where they had been stood. Tommy must have missed it, but he could then see somebody walking around the back of the car and moving towards the passenger door, before opening it and climbing in. The car then slowly moved away up the road.

"I never saw, I mean I never saw that person get out of the car," Tommy swore blindly to his friends.

Zain had pushed through under the bush and now also had a pretty good view on the movements below. "I believe you, Tommy and I agree, nobody got out of that car. They must have been walking but not down the road because we would have seen them. They must have been coming up the field behind us or along through the woods at the side of us. All I know is we need to be more vigilant. We can spot the car or the van or even Pilcher, but until we get a good look at these guys, we need to be more careful."

"You said it, Zain. Now that you say it, Zain, what if they have stopped up the road and are coming back across the top? We better get moving." Tommy was on it and already crawling along on his knees towards the top field heading back towards the village. Charlie and Zain were a little dazed and then it clicked. They began to follow on their hands and knees and then gave in. Up on their feet they jogged past Tommy who was still crawling.

"Keep up, man!" Charlie whispered as he ran past.

The boys turned up the path and went along the ridge of the hill back towards the village. It had turned into a dark evening as the clouds were preventing any moonlight from breaking through so they were confident as they moved along that they could not be seen from below. They had thought it a good idea to head down the steps between the houses instead of heading to Sandy Lane, this would bring them out on the small estate around the back of Charlie's house. They could then use all of the little paths that cut through between the houses to remain out of view from the roads for as much as possible.

At the end of the last cut through was the main road in to Crich. Charlie's house was about fifty metres up the road and if the BMW had stayed on its original route it would come back this way towards the village centre. They crouched down at the end of the path leaning up against the stone walls on either side to gain as much cover as possible.

Zain had taken up position at the front and was busy looking up and down the road while Tommy was making sure that there was nobody on the path to their rear. Charlie was frantically searching through his pocket and finally pulled out a set of keys for his front door.

"Hang on, let's not have the same as we did on Sunday. Let me find the door keys first so we are ready when we get there. Oh, and don't barge in again, my mum will be in is that clear? OK? Ready when you are."

Zain gave the all-clear and the boys ran down the road. The street lights flashed past quickly, light to dark, light to dark. The changing light was starting to make Charlie feel like he was on the sea, travelling over the waves, and an element of nausea came over him. Their footsteps could be heard down the road but at this point they didn't care; it was all about getting in to the house and closing that door behind them in order to feel safe. A moment later they were there, and Charlie was opening the door.

"Oh, hello, boys, what are you all up to?" Charlie's mum was stood in the hallway with a cup of tea in her hand.

"We've got this history task to finish off, Mum and thought it better to work here for a bit. Do you mind if we use the dining room?" Charlie blurted out panting heavily.

"Not at all, it's nice to have you all in for a change. Now you mention history, I bumped into Mr Pilcher yesterday morning and he told me that if you wanted some information you should go and speak to him."

"Oh? Did you tell him we were doing a project, or did he ask you?"

"Well he asked me, Charlie, apparently you had been checking out the old buildings on the high street on Sunday morning. And he said that he hadn't seen you on Friday night and just wanted to know where you were. You know what he's like anything happening in the village and he wants to make sure it's all going well. Anyway, please don't make too much noise, your sister has just gone to bed and boys nine o'clock is the latest tonight and then you are off home, understand?"

Mrs Cooper headed on through to the living room as the boys sat down in the dining room around the table. They waited until the living room door had closed to.

"What's Pilcher doing talking to your mum about us, has he ever done that before?" asked Tommy when he thought that Charlie's mum was far enough out of earshot.

"No, well not that I know of. He is suspicious of us though, but that's my opinion. I'm sure that he is on to us and he wants to find out how much we know. He must be something to do with those guys in that car, why else would he be asking Mum what we're up to?"

"What about the Burrowdale men?"

"Well the more I think about them it's more coincidence than anything, I think. Look at all the times we have seen them. So, they were up on Chadwick's Nick, maybe they were just passing through and had to stop for something. They were at the Cliffside Inn but so were a lot of people on Saturday night, they are related to the councillor maybe she was in there too. At the church they could have come to pick somebody up. I mean they never actually chased us, yes, they gave us a good old stare when we jumped over the wall but wouldn't you if you had been stood there and three lads came running out from behind a gravestone and legged it? In all honesty we probably looked dead suspicious."

"I see what you are saying about the Burrowdale men, let's keep an eye out for them though. Pilcher, that's paranoia, Charlie, don't you think he's just showing an interest and he's always been interested in the village history."

"I don't know any more, Tommy this stone is getting to me a bit, let's just get on with what we came here to do."

Zain had kept quiet throughout their discussion and was taking in all that they had said, and he was now siding with what Charlie was saying. It made sense about the Burrowdale men and it was only Mr Pilcher who was acting strange. He was now convinced that it was him that had been watching his house and had hidden away behind the houses when he himself had opened the curtains on Sunday morning.

Charlie reached over to the bookshelf in the corner of the room and found the large map of the surrounding area. He unfolded the pages and then became stuck flipping the map over from side to side and then finally, spinning it round one last time he pointed to Crich.

"Right, they don't make that easy do they, but here we are in Crich and the Merryweather Stone is down, here, look it's marked on."

"Well that's it. The stone turned and pointed in this direction." Charlie slowly drew his finger across the map from where the Merryweather Stone was in a line and rested it on to where the Memorial Tower stood. That's why the two guys were up there, they had clearly found out the same as we just have and had made their way over to see where to go next, they just couldn't go earlier because everybody was still there from the evening's gathering. Nearly everybody in the village had been there, you know what it's like, any stranger spotted, and everybody starts talking. Two guys rummaging around would have looked weird."

"They must have dropped the stone and couldn't stay any longer when the police arrived. We need to get back up to the Tor and see what they missed."

"Y'know the Merryweather Stone?" said Zain calmly, knowing that this was not going to go down well with his friends.

"Yeah," replied Tommy and Charlie, their heads turning slowly with suspicion.

"Well. You know it's not the only one, don't you?" Zain knew that they didn't.

"Zain are you kidding us, how long have you known that for?"

"Er? Well probably since I was about eight or nine."

"No! You muppet, did you not put two and two together? How many are there?"

"Well last I remember there are at least fifteen of them in the hills around here, I haven't been to all of them but when I was younger Mum and Dad used to take us out walking all over and we would always end up being shown something old. Give me until tomorrow and I can ask my dad where they all are. He'd be able to draw them all on for us."

"Oh, my word, your dad knows about all this too, you are beyond belief, man!"

"Oh, thank you," replied Zain.

"Hang on. We know where the Merryweather Stone is and it's marked on the map, maybe we can just find all of the others on the map with the same symbol." Charlie pulled the map over and started to look for Crich.

"No, it's not that simple, Dad said there are more, but they are not all real standing stones. Well I mean he said that some of them had been added at later dates so are not as old as the others. Look I'll take the map and go over it with Dad to get the details for us. OK?"

Zain folded up the map and placed it under his arm. It was getting close to nine o'clock so before Charlie's mum came through it was best to call it a day and get home. Not to mention the thought that his mates might be a bit upset with him and he didn't want to go through the grief that they would give him. Tommy thought it was a good time to call it a day too, so he and Zain said their goodbyes to Charlie at the door and agreed to knock on as usual for Zain in the morning. They stepped out onto the road and gave a check up and down to see if it was clear then made their way home.

Chapter Fifteen

Up at the Tor (Friday)

The boys had gotten together over their breaks at school and had decided on a plan of action for the evening.

Eight o'clock was late enough for the rest of the village to all be indoors. Nobody would be around now except the odd dog walker, but they mainly remained to the paths around the centre of the village and near to their homes. The sun had gone down about two hours ago and the moon was now bright in the sky breaking through the clouds as they blew along. The keeper in the cottage near the memorial would also be all locked up for the night and as long as they stayed away from his house, they would be good.

The journey to the edge of the village had been easy as they were now experts at keeping out of sight and remaining silent when it was required. Tommy had set the pace and it was like he was on a mission and had to get there as soon as possible. He had chosen to miss out Zain's field excursion tonight and they went through the park instead up to St Mary's church and then across the graveyard and on to the path that ran up towards the Memorial Tower.

Reaching the final hurdle, the boys decided to err on the side of caution and subsequently ended up sat inside what could only be described as one of the most stinky rooms they had ever been in. Despite having grown up in the countryside the smell of animal poo mixed in with

'Empty horse house'

wet straw and mud was a gross smell. The boys had noticed that the horses had been taken out of the field that lay below the war memorial and with the stall that they used for shelter being empty it gave the boys a great place to get their thoughts together before they made their way up to the top.

Charlie had for a long time thought that he liked these small little huts that were dotted around the fields about Crich but had never been in one. Now that he had experienced it, he had come to the conclusion that he liked the look of them but not being in them. He wasn't now sure what he had just put his foot in either and it was starting to bother him.

"Lads, if we are ready it might be good to get started, we still don't know where to place the rune and it could take us some time to search the tower."

"Good point, mate." Tommy had been peeping through a small hole in the wall where at some point one of the stones had either crumbled away or had been knocked out. There was a hedge on the outside so nobody was sure how much Tommy could actually see but it made him feel as though he was doing something really important, so nobody asked any questions.

Tommy had the plan to get up to the top though. "I say this time we just go straight up the road, it's quick and if anybody comes, we jump over the hedge, and then, well you know what to do then, run! Oh yeah and stay away from the keeper's house, he used to have a dog."

And that was it, tonight for Tommy it would appear there was going to be no messing around. They pulled out of their hiding place and in a moment of stupidity or confidence they walked along the road. They knew no cars would be coming, the real danger was being seen by people who were coming towards them.

"This is much better, eh, lads?" It was half question and half statement, but Tommy had widened his stride and was almost marching them up the hill. At this rate if anybody did come, they would not have the energy to run.

"Slow it down a bit would you, Tommy, we're going to be knackered before we get there," Charlie said concerned they may not see somebody in front of them if they were going too fast.

"Sorry, lads it's the adrenalin kicking in, I just want to be up there and find the next clue."

The march slowed slightly but it was still a quicker ascent than Charlie and Zain had imagined. They were both becoming out of breath just in order to keep up with Tommy. They were here now though, and they had to stay together! Charlie's senses were becoming overloaded as he was trying to keep an eye out both in front on his friend and behind him to make sure that nobody was following them.

"Zain, wait!" Charlie had stopped and was peering back down the road that they had just walked along. "Is that? Did that?"

"What is it, Charlie? Don't do this to me now."

Charlie continued to stare down the road, straining his eyes to see into the darkness. "It's OK. It must just be paranoia. I had that feeling, you know that somebody was behind me and then when I looked, I thought that I had seen something, not a cat or fox, something bigger, moving over the road and in to the bushes, down there on the right. I've had this feeling for the last few days. It's like somebody is always watching me, like somebody is always there but they are just out of sight, hidden, waiting, watching."

Zain looked back down the road but could not see anybody or any sign of movement. "Hey, it's like you say. Paranoia. We are expecting people to follow us, so your mind is starting to play tricks on you. I don't see anything. C'mon, let's catch up with Tommy."

A few moments later the boys reached the Memorial Tower in double time. It looked more ominous in the dark than it had ever felt before, reaching upwards to the sky. Charlie was feeling slightly dizzy as he looked up. It didn't help being near to the cliff edge, even though he knew his feet were firmly on the ground and there was no way he could fall. They picked up where they had left off earlier in the week except this time, they had more of an idea of what to look for. They flitted from wall to wall that stood around the tower and then focused on the tower itself.

After about ten minutes their search had been fruitless, and they were starting to feel disheartened.

Tommy had stopped altogether and was tired of searching again. His attention had turned to the sign that gave the information about the history of the Memorial Tower. As he started to read it the truth became clear.

"Guys, they got it wrong and so have we! We all presumed that it was the tower that we were looking for."

"Tommy stop mucking about, man what do you mean?"

"It says here on this plaque that the original tower was moved to this site in 1923 when the quarrying started to get too close. Well don't you get it? There must be another way marker up here, another stone, you know like the Merryweather Stone. We just assumed it was the Tor because it's in the same place. When you think about it this wouldn't have been here eight or nine hundred years ago would it?"

"But there's nothing up here that big, Tommy, people would have known about it."

"Yeah but what if it's partially buried from rubble that they dug up from the quarrying or from when they were building?"

Zain and Charlie looked at each other and knew that Tommy was on to something. They changed their approach and fanned out around the tower looking for something that could be a large standing stone that was at least half buried.

Charlie had already checked several mounds around his side of the tower and had stopped to decide which order to tackle the next few. He had moved down the hill slightly and was now stood in one of the old overgrown pits. It was then when he moved his foot that he noticed that one of his feet was resting on a flat rock. He moved his foot to one side and crouched down. His foot had been slightly covering a small circular indentation. Could this be the stone he had been looking for?

"Tommy, Zain over here!"

They came running over and stopped by his side.

"I think this might be it." They were slightly confused when he had said this as they could see nothing, and it was only when he started to tap his foot on the floor that they twigged on to what he was getting at.

Zain knelt down next to Charlie's foot. "Step aside then." He reached into his inside coat pocket and pulled out the rune stone. He looked at both of his friends. Their eyes had become wide and expectant. Tommy was nodding with encouragement, so he did it.

Zain reached down to place the rune stone into the shallow groove.

"Wait," Charlie called out. "You know what this means, lads. If this works, we are on the next step and that means that we are in it until the end. There will be no stopping us. Are we all agreed?"

Tommy spoke up first. "It's been agreed since day one, Charlie, I'm not going to let you do this one without me."

Zain held the rune stone out in front of him. The moon came out from behind a cloud and its light hit the stone creating a halo effect along the stone's outer edge. At that moment Zain believed that he could feel the magical power within the rune, a surge of energy running through his body. It was more likely to be excitement but to him it was mystical. He tried to think of something prophetic but failed dismally. "You bet, Charlie."

He reached his arm downwards again but this time he was not interrupted. He gently placed the rune stone in to the shallow hole and paused. He started to count in his head, *One, two, three, four yes!*

In the darkness the rune stone could barely be seen, its outline only visible when the moon came out briefly from behind the clouds again. The rune stone had started to rotate. "Clockwise, man it's clockwise again!" This time its movements were smoother and more definite.

Tommy reached over and placed his hand on Zain's shoulder. "Clockwise, man. You did it again, Zain. I say from now on you always place the rune stone down. I think you've got the touch."

"When you two have done falling in love, which way is it pointing?"

Zain had been distracted by his friend and needed to refocus his eyes on the dark stone that was on the ground in front of him. For a rounded object it was still easy to get the direction. When he had taken in the information, he instinctively knew that he had to refuse to go, especially now.

"Oh, man, no way, OK. We are not doing that! Not tonight!" Zain lifted his right arm up and pointed out past the fence and into the darkness. "Charlie, we are not going on to the moor in the night, man that's a bad idea. It'll have to be tomorrow morning. I know I literally just said we stick together but that is just stupid to go out there at night without some proper planning and equipment."

Tommy and Charlie had looked along Zain's arm and followed the direction that he was pointing. There was no point straining their eyes as it was pitch dark. Moorwood Moor lay before them. Several miles of moorland with little or no buildings, houses or people. They had all been there at some point in their lives with their families on walks, but it was not a place, like Zain had said, to venture lightly.

"Zain, Zain, it's okay, mate, I hear your words and I agree. There is no way we should go out there tonight. I mean nothing would probably happen but if it did, we would be in serious trouble. I just can't believe this is happening. Tommy bring that compass of yours over here we need to get a heading so that we can plot it on the map when we get home. That will save us from having to come back up here tomorrow morning." Charlie had recalled his training from Scouts.

Tommy passed the compass to Charlie so that he could take an accurate reading on which direction the rune stone was guiding them. "I think that we've been here long enough don't you? Maybe we should head off before anybody sees us and starts to take notice of what we are up to."

"Agreed, let me just make a note of this and then we are done." Charlie scrambled around in his pocket for a piece of paper and the pen that he knew he had somewhere. He could feel the pressure of the others wanting to go. Finally, there it was. He took a good look at the compass and noted the reading. He picked up the rune stone and passed it to Zain for safekeeping.

"That's yours to protect, Zain, let's go."

'Towards Moorwood Moor'

The boys gathered their stuff making sure to collect everything. It would be a shame to leave something that could lead the others to them.

Tommy stood next to Charlie as Zain was just checking that he hadn't dropped anything around the front of the Memorial Tower. "Hey, Charlie. That was like that possessed stuff right. He was like one of those witch doctors you know who use these runes to tell the future."

Charlie checked that Zain was still far enough away to not hear him and quietly spoke to Tommy. "Well they're not witch doctors but I know what you mean. Keep an eye on him. He's said a few things recently that have, well you know, made me think. One of us may need to look after the rune stone for a while."

The journey home was uneventful, thankfully to all of them, another chase or sighting would have taken them over the edge. They were about to uncover the truth about the rune stone that they had discovered and to be scared one more time would possibly put them off taking that leap in the morning. When they reached Zain's, Charlie made sure that Zain still had the rune stone. "Make sure it's safe tonight because without it tomorrow morning we are not going anywhere."

Tommy and Charlie made their way across the marketplace and parted.

"Take care, mate. Still miss Norwich?"

"It had its moments, but this has been something completely different. You've been a good friend to me, Charlie, I don't think I could have made it had I not met you."

"Hey, it's cool, there's been times that you've been the only one I can speak to as well. I think we need to be there for Zain now though. This is exciting but it seems to be overwhelming for him. I never thought to ask him about it before today so let's look out for him, agreed?"

"You're on. He's one of us and I know what you mean. I thought we were having fun but he's changing. Like you said earlier, that rune stone might need to come to one of us after tomorrow. I know you didn't want it, so I don't mind. I can hide it well enough if you want."

"Okay. I've got some stuff that I need to do before I meet up with you guys in the morning and I need to get a few things together too, make sure you bring your gear, food, water and stuff just in case we are out there for a while."

———————

When Charlie reached home, he checked in with his mum to make sure that she was okay. Sally had been watching the tv and was glad to see Charlie home at a reasonable time for a change.

"Hey, Charlie, how are you? Good evening?"

"Yeah, it's been really good thanks, Mum.

"Mum I'm tired I'm going to head up to bed okay?"

"Oh. Charlie wait, are you okay?"

"Yeah, I mean yeah sure. All's good. I just need to get some stuff ready for the morning before I go to sleep."

As he went out of the room, he grabbed the map from the bookshelf and looked back at his mum. "We're thinking of going for a hike in the morning, Mum is that okay?"

Sally looked up at Charlie. "Of course it is, just make sure you write down where you are going so I know but I'll see you for breakfast?"

"Yeah, an early breakfast though, I'm meeting somebody at 9:00." Charlie couldn't help but give a small smile.

"Oh, oh I see, and are you expecting to be back for lunch?"

"Yeah possibly, wait, I mean yes for breakfast, but I was going to take some sandwiches with me. Can we have our dinner later in the evening? Wouldn't want to miss out on a nice dinner. This is the one weekend in four that we don't have company."

"OK you're on. Might let you choose a film this time. You can tell me all about her when you get home. You're still my boy and I know when something is going on, Charlie. Anyway, night, Charlie." His mum gave him a knowing smile.

Charlie quickly headed upstairs before his mum started to ask any embarrassing questions, got ready for bed and jumped in. He picked up the map and took out the piece of paper that he had written the compass reading on. It was second nature now to find the Memorial Tower on the map. He spun the map around on his pillow and placed the compass back on top. He moved it around to match up with the reading that he had taken. He aligned the map and compass, it pointed directly into the middle of the moor.

Good place to hide something, he thought.

He stretched over to his desk and grabbed a ruler and pencil and attempted to draw a line on the map which was easier said than done as he rested on the soft pillow.

He lifted his head to get a better view of the map and pencil line he had just drawn. It ran along to the moor and out over the stone circle.

That has to be it, the circle has been there long enough, and nobody would move that.

The circle was seldom visited, in fact you had to have permission to go to it as it was on private land owned by one of the farms. There was though a small path that led to it and as far as he knew the farmer was okay with people going over the edge of his field as long as you didn't trash it. Not many people knew that though.

He looked over the map at where Mr Talpur had put a few pencil marks identifying locations of the standing stones that he knew about. He was looking to see if there was a pattern, but he could not see anything. They appeared to be placed randomly around the landscape. They didn't even tie up with the tops of hills or anything like that.

Charlie's finger moved around the map from pencil mark to pencil mark checking out all of the places that he knew. Had he been to these stones or did he know of the paths that would lead him there? Apart from the ones close to Crich the answer to both questions he found was 'No'. His finger continued to move around the page and then stopped. He read the words next to the symbol showing an outcrop of rocks. 'Shuck Rock'. A shiver ran over him. Despite being in his bed under the duvet he was now cold. That story had been told to him on many occasions and it was not one he liked to re-call. The images filled his mind, the fur black as night, its eyes red with fire and fangs yellow dripping with drool.

Before today he had not really believed all of that which he had been told about the legend. There were several stories in circulation of how people had come across the Shuck out in the Moors, others told of how it had come to find them all of which ended in tragedy.

'Shuck Rock', this is one thing not to tell the others in the morning. They don't need to know about that unless we need to go near it.

The fear was building in him and he needed to find something to take his mind off it. He took one last look at the map and folded it away into his rucksack next to his bed.

Charlie's thoughts turned to meeting up with Ali in the morning. He was slightly afraid of the outcome of that meeting too as he wanted it to work out, but that fear was ten times better than the thought of meeting with the 'Shuck'.

Chapter Sixteen

It's a Date! (Saturday Morning)

Charlie awoke with a start. He almost jumped in his bed. He looked around from where he lay with his head on his pillow to see if something had happened to wake him so abruptly, but nothing appeared to be amiss. He could feel that his body was sweaty, he must have been having another bad dream but could not re-call it. His plans for the day started to fill his mind.

Charlie was well aware that he had made plans with Zain and Tommy and he had to be there prompt. Zain's house was only around the corner so it shouldn't be a problem. This was it though he was also going to meet up with Alison first. It may only be for a quick drink, maybe something to eat but he would wait to see what else she had to say. He had to crack on, lots to do today, he thought.

————————

Nervous was not the word for it. He had really liked her, 'love' however was a word that he may have used himself, but he had never said it to her. Charlie had arrived at the café first and had taken a moment to choose the table that he thought would give them the best privacy. At the moment the café was empty, but he knew that shortly it would start to fill up with parents and their kids coming in for a late breakfast or an early lunch.

"Morning, Mr Barnet, how are you?" Charlie had been in the café a million times and everybody knew Mr Barnet around the village.

"Yep, you know how it is, Charlie, bit early for you isn't it? You're not bringing that idiot in today, are you?"

Charlie gave a little chuckle. "No, no Tommy's not coming in today, well erm, not with me anyway. He doesn't mean any harm, Mr Barnet he's a good lad really, he just likes to play about. I'm meeting somebody else today." Charlie looked away quickly as the nerves kicked in again.

"Oh. Ohhh, I see." He gave a quick nod and a wink. "Well you let me know if I can help out. Just give me a shout, OK?"

Charlie thought about how this time last week he was waking up on Tommy's bedroom floor having found the rune stone the night before. It had been a long week, well it felt that way to him. The door to the shop opened and drew him from his thoughts. Charlie knew that it was her. He turned slowly and smiled in Alison's direction. "Hey, how you doing?"

"Good thanks, Charlie, how are you?"

"Good yeah. Honestly? I'm feeling nervous. I'm not blaming you, but I don't, I don't want to get hurt again, Ali." Charlie had not wanted to start off this way but deep down he needed to be assured that he was not going to be wasting his time chasing what he could not have, and he wanted to protect himself. It had truly been painful for him the last few months.

"I'm sorry, Charlie I don't know how it ended up the way it did. It was like we or I didn't have a choice. Can we sit down and get a drink?"

"Of course we can. I thought this would be good." Charlie gestured towards the table by the window. He made his way over to the table and threw his rucksack on the floor next to it. Alison grabbed the nearest chair which also gave her the view out of the window. Charlie had hoped that he would have been able to face that in case Tommy came bumbling along the path. That way he would have been able to spot him first, but hey. He sat down at the table.

"Well I think I might get a cup of tea and maybe a couple of crumpets for breakfast or shall we get a few more and share?" Charlie was always up for a cup of tea and would rather have had that than a fizzy drink.

"Yeah let's share as long as we can have some jam with them. I didn't eat much before I came out you know. I get nervous too."

Charlie called for Mr Barnet who promptly appeared through the beaded ribbons that covered the doorway as though he had just been hovering, waiting to be called upon. Possibly, or more likely he had been listening in on their conversation. They placed their order which was also delivered in double quick time. They started to talk about what they had both been up to over the last few months and how they had both missed seeing each other. The crumpets had gone down a treat and things were going well in Charlie's mind. Alison looked happy and she was hinting at wanting to meet up later in the week.

Charlie was feeling happier than he had for a long time just being there with Alison was all that he had really wanted. The stuff that was going on with his mates was great. His mates! Charlie looked at the clock on the wall and realised that it was nearly ten o'clock. He had to be at Zain's in a few minutes. He wanted to go but at the same time he wanted to stay and be with Alison. He needed to make his excuses and quick.

"Hey. I need to go and see Zain and Tommy we've got to go and do something. It's quite important and I can't let them down, not today. Would it be alright if we meet up again though?"

Alison was curious as to where he had to go at ten in the morning in Crich but didn't ask him. Not today. Charlie was looking at Alison waiting for her response but by the look of the expression on her face something had caught her attention outside.

Oh no, not Tommy! She was clearly now focused on whatever it was going past outside the shop. *Please don't be Tommy*, he thought. He didn't need that level of interruption right now.

"Well that is one thing I have never seen before. I've just watched a van go by with the biggest dog I have ever seen, hanging its head out of the window. It must have been as big if not bigger than an adult man. It was taking up the whole seat. Its tongue was even flapping in the wind, like slapping side to side." Alison was holding her hand next to her mouth and flapping her hand up and down mimicking what she had just seen.

"Oh, sorry, Charlie that was rude of me, it just took me by surprise. That was a massive dog, I hope they can control it. Later this week yeah, sure I'd like that, I'd say tonight but I'm meeting up with Emma we're having a sleepover."

Charlie was slightly taken aback by that comment. He didn't know that they were close friends, well especially enough to hang out and have a sleepover. Now he thought about it he was trying to think of everything that he had said to Emma in class. Had he said anything bad about Alison? Oh no, this was worrying him. Time was up he had to go. He would have to leave it at this and hope that Alison would meet up with him again.

"Alison, I need to get off. Thanks for meeting with me today. I've… well. It's been really nice just spending time with you." He reached over the table and placed his hand on to hers. What was he thinking, that was too soon, Charlie!

"You too, Charlie."

They walked over and stood on the doorstep of the café and looked at each other. Charlie knew this was the time to do it. He leant in towards Alison and gave her a kiss on the cheek. He could smell her perfume and the memories of their time together came rushing back to him.

"I'll call you later?" said Charlie.

"Please do, Charlie, don't let me down."

Alison turned around and made her way down the street back towards her home. Charlie stood there almost not believing what had just happened. If he played it 'right' he could be together with Alison again and this time he would not let others interfere with his relationship. This was going to be difficult though not to tell his friends, but he had to make it work.

Mr Barnet reappeared by the counter. "Nice work there, young man," he said smiling.

"You better believe it, the Charlster still has it!"

Charlie realised what he had just said and was so embarrassed. He handed some money to Mr Barnet and held his head down in shame hoping that he would never repeat it to anybody. When he saw Zain, he was going to give him some grief for ever planting that stupid name in his head. Charlie made his way out of the café and could just about make out Ali farther down the road. He watched her walk down the street for a few seconds and then put on a quick jog along the path in the opposite direction to get to his friends on time.

Chapter Seventeen

A Cold Walk to Shuck Rock (Saturday)

The journey from Crich to the stone circle was a little over two miles. Charlie had a rough idea of where it was, but he had never actually been there or even seen it as it was concealed from view by the surrounding hills. The fog was as thick as they had ever seen it and up on the moorland it was hard to see any further than a few metres ahead and therefore easy to become disorientated. The boys could feel the damp air on their faces and the northerly wind that blew added to the chill.

Thinking about it, they were lucky with the weather, as nobody would be able to see them cross the fields.

The boys had made it all the way along the road to where the farmyard started. The footpath through was on the other side of the road so they decided to take stock of what they were about to do and make sure they were all on the same page if anything was to happen.

They peeked up above the wall that they had been sat behind and took one final look around to make sure that they were not being followed. The last thing that they wanted was to bump into the two men or the Burrowdale men in the open moor. Zain checked his pocket again to make sure that the rune stone was still there. He knew that it was, because he had checked at least ten times in as many minutes.

The start of the path was quite wide, more like a narrow track. It had clearly been driven down by the farmer in his tractor as the tyre tread marks had cut into the wet mud at some point down either side. Large puddles stretched out in front of them and the boys found themselves jumping from one side of the path to the other trying to avoid standing in the puddles or going into the deep mud. Before they knew it, the path had shrunk down in size as they entered the grass fields and it now became nothing more than a faint line where the grass was darker than that which surrounded it. This was a seldom used path thought Charlie.

With the fog as it was apart from the ground it was like walking into a bright white light. Avoiding the puddles had been a pointless exercise as after a few metres the amount of dew and water that was on the long grass had soaked in to their boots and trousers. Zain was not impressed as he had foolishly worn his jeans which were becoming uncomfortable.

Charlie had estimated it to be about another mile from where they were to the circle and they should just be able to follow the path through the fields and look out for the turn off when they got a bit closer. In Charlie's memory it was quite a distinctive little knoll that stuck up by the side of the track, however, he had not counted on the fog being so thick and hoped that they would not miss it.

The trek was taking longer than expected as it was difficult to navigate in the thick fog. Concentrating on looking in front, so they didn't walk into something, meant the boys kept stumbling on bumps along the ground. The moor was a strange place to be. When the sun shone, and the sky was blue, it was absolutely beautiful. Today, it took on a different feel. The moor felt empty. They had not seen anybody since walking through the centre of the village and now on the moor they had not heard a single thing other than their footsteps and groans. That silence was about to be broken.

"Could have sworn I just heard a dog growl." Tommy had stopped and was looking into the white cloud behind them.

Charlie's heart skipped a beat as he heard the words come from Tommy's mouth. It couldn't be he thought. They had now all stopped and were straining their ears and eyes to take in anything that hinted at the presence of somebody or something else on the moor with them.

"C'mon, there's nothing there."

No sooner had he said it than the faint sound of a dog growling floated through the clouds to their side. It wasn't close they knew that, but it was difficult to judge any real distances. Charlie was convinced that it was to his left and then Zain pointed out in front of him.

"There! It came from over there this time."

Meanwhile Tommy had been looking in the opposite direction and was convinced that the noise was coming from in front of him too.

"This is not right, guys It's all around us," Zain stated.

"Stand your ground and stick together that's the best thing for us to do, okay?"

"Holy crap! What was that?"

The boys froze to the spot. The noise was still echoing around them. A sharp and piercing howl had just come through the fog. It was a harrowing sound that was full of pain and it was like nothing the boys had experienced before this day.

"I don't like it, guys, that's not natural!" By now Zain had backed up into his two friends.

"Me neither. I never believed it when they told me about the Shuck but of all the places to start hearing those sorts of noises. It can't be true." Charlie could not hold it in any longer and let out what he had been keeping secret from the others.

The howling began again and this time it was closer. It wasn't easy to tell from which direction it had come as the sound was being carried through the fog surrounding them. Despite being in the open it all began to feel a little claustrophobic.

"What are you on about 'Shuck'? You said that the other day at the church."

Tommy paused for a second as a sudden shiver ran down his body.

"Oh, Charlie, what have you not told us, man?"

The words came slowly from Charlie's mouth as he explained. Tommy knew that his friend was afraid of something and was trying his hardest not to show it on his face as he turned towards him.

"At this exact moment, Tommy, it might not be best for you to find out what the Shuck is. Trust me, Tommy, you don't want to know but I know you will just keep asking me and if I don't tell you. Well. The Shuck, they say is tall and vile with red eyes and yellow teeth. That's the saying that we have always been told. It's a local legend that tells of a fiendish hound its fur as dark as the night, that lives in the rocky outcrops around Matlock."

"Well that would be about where we are!" Tommy interrupted him.

"Yeah I know b…b…but I didn't want to say it myself. The stories say that it's one of those omen things you know, if you see it, well it means that somebody is going to die."

"Yeah, well, you don't believe all that sort of stuff, do you? Cos we'd know about that and somebody would have seen it and all that." Tommy was now trying hard to convince his own mind that it was not real.

Another howl and growl came from behind them. They all spun around instantly and closed in towards each other.

Charlie carried on a little quieter than before. "That's what the tales say, Tommy, I mean it's all just stories." He looked at his friends, raised his eyebrows and gave them both a smile. It wasn't fooling them.

Just being told the story up here on a day like today would get the imagination playing tricks on you and combined with the noises that they were hearing it was enough to give Tommy and Zain the shivers, they were both starting to look more nervous. Each of them tried to look in to the fog but it was no use, the Shuck could have been ready to pounce directly behind them and they would never have seen it until it was too late, literally.

"You can stop leaning on me now, Zain," exclaimed Tommy.

"I'm not leaning on you it was erm, one of those defensive tactical things where you all put your backs together that way you can see in every direction. Alright?"

The boys had been stood there for some time now and signs were starting to show that the cold was taking effect on them. Each of them, was beginning to shiver. Charlie could feel that his arms and legs were starting to go stiff from being stood still for a period of time. There had not been a significant noise in the past ten or fifteen minutes. They were not totally sure how long it had actually been but that was their rough estimate.

"We've got to move on, guys. If we stay here, we are going to freeze!" Charlie whispered.

"Good grief, man! Would you tell me the next time you are going to speak! You scared the heck out of me!"

Zain had never been the most confident and today had really taken him to the edge of his comfort zone and well beyond. Not many people had their own tale of the Shuck to tell and this would be a cracker if they got the chance to re-tell it; it would be enough to give anybody a fear of the moor.

"Agreed, I haven't heard anything for ages now, it must have gone. We should head back," said Tommy.

"But we've come so far, and I know that we are close, Tommy. Ten more minutes and we should be there."

Despite his fears Charlie was determined to get to the end today.

The boys walked on slowly straining their eyes to look into the fog to see if they could see anything. Finally, it seemed that the fog was thinning up ahead, the whole sky around them was becoming brighter. As they moved onwards the sky started to change from a dark grey into a beautiful orange and through the mist, they could see the sun like a bright disk in the sky. This change filled them with confidence and they no longer felt so far away from home. It had also started to warm up, only slightly but again this was enough to give them a little security. Zain was back on form and had reached in to his back pack and was munching on a Jaffa Cake.

It had been at least half an hour since they had heard the last howls and they had not seen anything moving around them much to their relief. It was at this point that they actually stumbled upon the hillock that led off towards the stone circle that they had been searching for.

"Oh. Look, lads this must be it, not quite what I was expecting, thought it was going to be bigger." Tommy was clearly not impressed.

They couldn't quite yet see all of the circle from where they were but as they reached the first stone the formation could be made out more clearly. Each of the stones was casting a shadow that made the circle look like it was leaning at an angle. This was slightly disturbing on the eye to start with but as they moved around it became the normal.

"We need to find the right stone, right?" Tommy had already started to count the stones as his head went up and down moving round the circle.

"It must work in the same way as the other markers. Look around the stones to see if any of them have an indentation or hollow that the rune stone will fit into."

Charlie was getting excited and wanted to know what would come next, what they would find or what direction they would need to move in. Tommy and Zain split off and went in different directions around the circle stopping at each of the stones and investigating.

Meanwhile Charlie had started to survey the surroundings and was looking at the layout of the circle in front of him. He could see the other two crouching by stones at the far side of the circle rubbing their hands around the stones to see if they could feel anything that resembled the indentations that they had found at the previous sites.

This is too obvious, he thought. *Hang on, the circle was here a thousand years before the Norsemen trekked across the land. Surely, they wouldn't have interfered with a stone circle, they would have held respect for such sites.*

With this in his mind Charlie turned and looked behind him and walked a little bit out from the circle. He started to walk around the circle itself going in a clockwise direction. If they didn't touch the circle, they may have placed something nearby in order to make it blend in and possibly give it some protection from others choosing to remove or damage it.

Sure enough, standing alone was a solitary stone around ten metres away from the main circle. Charlie thought that it was looking a little worse for wear, half covered in moss and leaning at an unbelievable angle. In fact, he was surprised that it was still holding itself up. From the direction in which Charlie was standing, combined with where he thought he was, this stone, the Tor and the circle would make a straight line.

"Guys, I think that I have it over here," Charlie called out to Tommy and Zain.

He placed his hands on the stone and moved them slowly around. There it was a clear indentation that had been carved, although again it was now smooth with the years of erosion.

By now the fog had really started to lift, the sun burning through the cloud to warm their faces. The surrounding landscape was being revealed to them too, familiar hills and the farm behind them, which was just in sight. Their confidence grew slightly as they did not feel as isolated as before, but they were still wary having just encountered 'The Beast of Lumsdale'.

———————

"I'm worried about the angle of this stone it's nowhere near upright!" stated Charlie.

"I know what you mean. We're just going to have to give it a go and hope that it works."

Zain passed the rune stone to Charlie. He held it in his hand. This was the first time that he had really held it since the night that he had found it. It was heavier than he recalled, darker too. "We agreed that it would be you who would place the rune stone in, Zain. I'm not going to break that now." He passed the rune stone back to his friend.

Zain swapped places with Charlie and placed the rune stone onto the top of the stone and balanced it as best he could. They all watched, holding their breath.

The rune started to move, slowly scratching its way as it began to spin clockwise.

"It still works, look at that it's pointing that way back towards..." Charlie stopped mid-sentence as he knew that his friends would not wish to know where the rune now directed them.

Solemnly he spoke. "The only thing in that direction that I know of, lads, is Shuck Rock."

"You have got to be kidding me? I didn't think that I would ever say this, but I believe it. All the stories that I have ever heard, I believe it, man." Zain had not taken this news well and was being serious, the tone in his voice showed that he was fearful of what it now meant.

If they were to go any further with finding out what all this was about, they would have to face those fears and cross the short strip of moors to Shuck Rock. A breeze had started to blow over the field which picked up the remaining wisps of mist. On the hillside across the field they could see the lone outcrop of rock.

———————

Billy Burrowdale was fighting to hold on to the two hounds that he had just walked around the moor. Hounds would be the only word to describe them, some would say they compared to small ponies in size, but they were definitely canine. The sheer size of them would put them in good stead to fight off anything that they were not happy with, the drool dripping from their faces was only natural, but it gave them a fierce and unholy look. Meeting something like that in the fog or dark would not be the best way to spend your day. Especially if you combined that with the look of Billy Burrowdale, who was a good six-foot-tall or more, and had done lots of physical exercise or at some point had worked out in the gym.

"C'mon, boys. Here! In! In!" Billy was trying to be as assertive as he could with the dogs but once on their leads they just loved to be out and getting them back in the van was a real mission. Divide and conquer was his normal strategy, stick one in the back and the other would jump up on the seat next to him in the front. It had to wear a seat belt it was that big and it always got the window seat. He tried it in the middle, but it had nearly made them crash as it tried to tear its way out in order to get its head out of the window.

Brian Burrowdale on the other hand was the shorter of the two brothers but he had the brains, he was also the eldest of the brothers, so in some sense got to call a lot of the shots between the two. He was stood leaning against the side of the van and had offered no help to his brother in trying to get the dogs back in the van.

"Well, did anybody see you?" asked Brian.

"Nope. I took a good walk around though, down by the circle and over to Shuck Rock then back again. Those three lads from the church were over by the stone circle but when they heard the dogs here it put the creepers up them, couldn't see them after that and din't want to get too close, but they probably legged it back towards the village."

"I tell you what, Billy, it's bloody brilliant how you trained that dog to do that. I'm still amazed by it."

Billy reached over to the dog to his left and placed his hand under its chin. He looked it in the eyes and blew gently on to its nose. The noise was even more horrifying at close range. The dog gave out a blood curdling howl and then its tongue dropped out of the side of its mouth as Billy gave his head a good rub. Billy had reached into his pocket and pulled out a piece of cooked liver.

"Here you go, boy, well done."

"Billy, when you say they were by the circle, could you see what they were doing?" asked Brian.

"Well in and out of the fog it was difficult to see, but they were just walking around the stones. It just looked like some sort of game, you know following each other around and one of them was jogging around the outside."

"Trust me on this, Billy, kids nowadays don't play games like that, I think we may need to keep an eye on them from now on. When we get back to the yard I want to see if we can find out who they are." Brian's voice had turned serious.

"Well that's easy, the tall one, well his dad brings his car in so we should have their records back at the garage."

Brian gave his brother a smug grin. "I like it, that makes life easier for us then. Dig it out and find the address. I think that we may need to give him a visit at some point."

Billy and Brian strolled around to the side of the van and both climbed in through the driver's door. Billy then clambered over into the middle seat next to his dog. Its head dropped and brushed against his chest lovingly.

'Shuck Rock'

Chapter Eighteen

The Next Clue

The final trek was about eight hundred metres across the field towards what Charlie and Zain knew as Shuck Rock. This was not one of their happiest moments. The fog was starting to thicken again ahead of them as it rolled down the hillside. Of all directions for the rune stone to have guided them this one would lead them closer to where other people had said that the Shuck had been sighted. Now Charlie had seen this rock before but had never been over to it. He recalled his dad wanting to go there when he was younger, but Charlie had been too scared and having made a fuss his dad had turned them around and had gone back. That was one of the last memories Charlie had of his dad before he left.

The rock itself was nothing much to look at, a slightly darker grey than the usual rocks, and it had moss growing around its base. Okay, maybe it was slightly larger than the others that stood out on the moor but not excessively. This rock though was solitary as the others tended to be in small groups of rocky outcrops and it was positioned on a slight rise in the surrounding ground. As they approached their pace slowed, all of them, heads swaying side to side, checking their surroundings for any signs of people or beastly hounds.

Tommy and Charlie could hear Zain whispering, he was still nervous. Charlie was too but he was trying not to show it. Charlie could see

Tommy's fingers going as his hands swung by his sides. He knew he was feeling the pressure too.

They slowly approached the stone, Charlie was out in front slightly, mainly thanks to Tommy's hand which was now on his shoulder holding Charlie in front of him at arm's-length, Zain following up at the rear was not too far from Tommy. Charlie stopped walking suddenly about five metres from the rock and the others could not react quick enough to stop, causing them to bump into one another.

"What is it, do you see something?" Tommy asked.

"No. Just wondered if anybody wanted to trade places."

"Not a chance, pal, you found the rune stone which means it's your fault we are all here. If a giant dog wants to sink its fangs in to anybody might as well be you, hey? Obviously, I'll miss you, but you know." Tommy gave him a gentle nudge and the boys moved on.

It was a strange desire but as Charlie advanced towards the rock, he held out his arm to touch the stone. He placed his hand firmly on the rock. It was damp and cold to his touch, but it did make him feel better about their situation.

"I think we're good, lads. There doesn't seem to be anything here." They cautiously fanned out around the rock circling around it until they met on the opposite side.

"Check it over, see if there is an indentation or any markings." Charlie was feeling better but still wanted to get out of there as quickly as they could.

Tommy was on it and before the sentence was finished, he was scampering up the far edge of the rock which would lead him up towards the top. He figured that there may be a dip on the top like the other stones, although this one was larger. As he pulled himself up onto the top of the rock, he could see that there was nothing there and if there had been it had long gone through erosion.

Charlie and Zain meanwhile were scouring the sides of the rock rubbing their hands over the stone to see if they could feel any slight markings when Zain called out.

"Charlie, Tommy, come and check this out!" They were both there in an instant. Zain was peering into what looked like a small gap. Shuck Rock was not one, but two rocks that were leaning against each other tightly, and it was only here at the very base out of sight and covered by the undergrowth where Zain had stopped, that it was noticeable.

"Step aside, Zain, I'll do it." Charlie could tell that this was as close as Zain was going to a dark hole in the ground. He reached into his pocket and pulled out a small torch and gave it a tap on the bottom to switch it on. He moved closer praying that nothing was looking back from inside. He shone the torch into the hole.

"Well it looks like it goes back about a metre but it's not going to be big enough for any of us to go in. But it could be big enough to hide something." Charlie knelt down. He could feel the wet coming through his trousers from the ground, but it didn't deter him. He shone the torch around to check out every corner of the hole. There towards the back he could see a small mound on the floor.

Charlie tried to reach in but could not. The only way to do this was to lay down. He hesitated for a moment and knew that he had to do it. He stretched his arm inside the hole until he could feel the mound under his fingertips. His face was pushed tight up against the rock. The ground inside was hard as he started to scratch away the dirt.

"Have you found something, Charlie, tell us what it is." Tommy was becoming impatient and was twitching. He had the feeling that he was being watched and could not help himself from constantly turning around to see if anybody was there.

"Give me a second, man, there's something in here I know there is, it's just difficult to get it, if only I had something that I could use to get the mud off." Charlie continued to scratch away with his fingertips. He could feel them starting to hurt as the dirt piled up under his fingernails. *There, what's that?* Charlie had felt a change in what he was touching. *That's a... a corner.*

"There's some sort of a box in here, let me get this corner dug out and then I might be able to pull it out."

He pushed his face further into the rock as he now tried to get some sort of leverage on the far side of the box in order to pull it out.

"It's moving!"

"C'mon, mate you can get it."

"That's it, step back, let me up." Charlie rolled over on to his back and sat up. In his hand was a small wooden box. It was nothing special and from the looks of it, it was not that old, well not old enough to be from the Viking times. The boys looked slightly puzzled by what they had found as they could not understand what was going on.

Zain took a good look at the box. "Charlie, that's it, don't worry about what it looks like this is what we have come for. You need to open it." Zain was staring at Charlie now and had started to make him feel uncomfortable. Charlie took a breath and looked back at Zain, as he brushed the dirt and pieces of wet grass from his front. "Here we go. It's been a week of madness, let's hope that this has all been worth it."

Charlie cleaned the dirt from around the sides of the box and flicked back the small metal clasp that came over the front of the box. He turned the box around towards his friends and opened it.

"Holy Moley, that has to be solid silver!" Tommy squeaked.

Charlie looked over the top of the lid. He could now see what Tommy was excited about. There, inside was a silver brooch about eight centimetres across. It was upside down to Charlie's eyes and despite being only made up of the outlines it looked to him like a man with a bag over his shoulder or back and then some sort of pickaxe in the other. It was beautiful to look at.

Zain had been stood patiently now with his back to Charlie. "Guess I was right. Treasure!"

"It's a beautiful little trinket isn't it?" The voice came through the fog and was the last straw for the three boys who were now about as scared as could be. Within the last half an hour they had just had a close encounter with the Shuck and that was not an event in your life to take lightly.

The three boys let out a series of shrieks that were piercing made even more shrill by the closeness of the white fog which had now closed in all around them again.

The shadow of a man came steadily walking towards them through the fog.

"Oh, Charlie, this is not fun anymore, mate, when can we go home?" Zain had reached his limit and he now just wanted to be at home sat on the sofa with his blanket, wrapped up watching the T.V. preferably with some chocolate. But that was not going to happen, he had to be brave and face this new fear with his friends.

"Stay close, Zain," Charlie said calmly. "Remember there are three of us and one of him. If it all goes pear-shaped, run fast, run as fast as you can back towards the village. It's so boggy that it won't take much to lose somebody, the fog will help too. I'll try to distract them as long as I dare. If you get split off from each other we can all meet up back at the farm gate, it's that way, okay?"

———————

"Wait!" the old man called out. "I'm not here to hurt you."

The boys stopped in their tracks and now that he had said it there didn't really seem to be any threat from the elderly man that stood between them and their way home. The old man wore a long coat. Underneath, a hooded top came up covering most of his head which cast a shadow over his face. His eyes were almost black to look at and his stare was piercing as his gaze moved from one boy to the next.

"I know what you have, boys, oh yes I've seen it before, although many, many years ago now was the last time. I bet it's still as shiny now as it was then and the same as the day it was made, that's what makes it so special, see? That little trinket that 'you' now have has had many previous owners and I suppose I was its keeper or guardian for want of a better word for well over twenty years. I believe it's time to let it go, time for somebody else to take responsibility. That by the way means you three. I'm getting tired of coming out here all the time to make sure it's safe. Tell me how you found your way." You could hear the relief in the old man's voice as though a great weight had been lifted from him.

Charlie took a step forward and cleared his throat. "It's, erm. Hang on, Mr Pilcher, is that you?"

"Who else did you think would know what was going on?"

Zain and Tommy both let out sighs of relief. "Do you mean it though, Pilcher! You're not here for any kind of trouble, are you?"

"No, no, Tommy, I mean it, but we do need to sort out a few formalities. An agreement, let's call it between you three, the brooch and the rune." It was a strange thing to say but it had been a weird day, so it was now a matter of going with whatever it was that came their way.

"Well it's a long story how we came by it I suppose but to make it short, somebody dropped it and we found it. I think we all now know why they have all been chasing us to get it back though," Charlie explained.

"Others would say that it was fate that the stone came into your possession it all depends on how you see the way that the world works," replied Pilcher.

The boys were now listening intently to Pilcher, Zain more than the others who had also appeared to overcome his fears and had stepped forwards a little.

"The stone you have there is one of four that I am aware of, they all look very similar in size and shape, colour, to what you have, but the runes are different. You know that they all have different meanings and powers? The one that you have there, stands for 'The Sons of Woden'. That mark is special too, but if you want to carry on with what you have started you will need to see or possess the others. That one only works here and without the others, well. You did well with the timing too. Today would probably have been the last day given that the moon has now passed its fullest. You would have had a long wait until the next full moon had you ever realised that it was linked."

Zain reached for the rune stone to check that he had it but instinctively pulled it out of his pocket and held it out in front of the three boys. He didn't show it to Pilcher but had held it clasped in his hand with his fist faced downwards only showing the back of his hand with the rune on the inside facing him.

"Ahh, good you even hold it correctly in order to give its protection over your companions, but I've told you, you don't need it with me. Listen carefully, you need to be on your guard now. Don't let anybody know that you have the stone or that you have seen the pendant. Search for the sign of the pendant and you should discover the next rune stone. I'll get this back to where it belongs." He moved quickly, faster than the boys thought that he could and before they knew it, he was holding the pendant.

As the boys stood, mouths wide open in shock that the brooch had just been taken from them so swiftly, Pilcher started checking the brooch out to make sure it was still in good condition. He was mumbling under his breath, but they could just about make it out.

"Hmm they were lucky to make it work though, full moon's passed you see, I didn't realise that it would still work this long afterwards, suppose I'll have to report that back." His face had pulled an inquisitive look, you could see his thoughts rolling over as he added this new piece of information to some long list of knowledge about the rune stone.

As the boys leant inwards to try and hear each of the words Pilcher spun back around and spoke out louder than before, almost making a declaration and startling them.

"You are now the defenders, believe it or not but the runes are not controlled by men or women but by another force. That stone in your hands, Zain came to you for a reason. This rune is a very important one, it has a meaning, well it tells us things if you understand? Its symbol represents heritage and tradition, but you could read it another way. It also tells of nobility and inheritance and it is the last one that most will focus on, that's the one that gets all of those glory hunters. They believe that they will find the lost treasure. Well they won't. Let me assure you it is well hidden and many have tried to find it and many have even completed the first challenge as have you but it is the next step that will take courage as there will be suffering along the way. If you are going to pursue this, it would benefit all of you to learn the ways and understand the meanings of the runes."

"Mr Pilcher. Wait, this is all for real, everything you are saying, you're not just having us on, are you? That's why you have been following us?" Charlie had to know the truth.

"Yes, Charlie. What, do you think I got to my age and couldn't see a big bright light shining through the sky? I was up on the Tor the night you found the rune stone, I saw you show it to your friends and from then on, I've been keeping tabs on you. It was only when I knew that I believed in you, all three of you that I came forward. Like the runes told me, here you are 'The Sons of Woden'. Understand that this is the path that you will now follow, and remember, you will need one another to succeed."

Pilcher took one last look at the silver brooch that he had taken from the boys and placed it away for safe keeping. "This has to go elsewhere now, lads to be checked over, but you will see it again. I will place it back here at Shuck Rock in due course and there it should remain until the next holder of the rune stone discovers it." He reached into a pocket deep inside his coat and pulled out a small leather bag tied together at the top. Mr Pilcher looked at the boys. "Are you sure you are ready and are willing to take this on?"

"We are, Mr Pilcher." Charlie spoke out before the others had a chance to ask a question.

Mr Pilcher pulled on the straps of the leather bag and loosened the neck. He placed his hand inside, his eyes moved and then he looked at each of the boys. He rummaged his hand around inside but did not look as though he was actually purposefully selecting anything. The boys could hear what sounded like stones clattering together inside the bag. As Mr Pilcher pulled out his hand he focused on Zain.

"A single stone shall answer the one question in your mind. This is for you." He did not look to check what he was offering to Zain but gave it willingly. Unless he had been feeling for something his selection from the bag had been completely random, well at least that's how it appeared to the boys.

"You will understand its meaning eventually, and you will keep it safe, in turn your friends will keep you safe. The runes have chosen you and this is the one that will guide you now to the next stage. If they have spoken truthfully you will succeed if not you will spend your time in waste and will find only emptiness."

He held out his hand and Zain did the same. Mr Pilcher placed a stone into his hand which Zain quickly grasped tightly shut to shield the gift from view.

Mr Pilcher tied the bag tightly closed again with the leather straps and placed it back into his jacket pocket.

Zain could feel the object in his hand, and straight away he knew it was a rune stone of sorts. But why had Pilcher selected him to give it to? He couldn't know that he had looked after the first rune, could he? The stone was smooth like the first, however, this was much colder and smaller, maybe from being in Pilcher's pocket, he would have to find out in time. He rolled it over in his palm and then his fingers found the shape of the rune that had been carved. It was different there was no doubt in that. Zain's fingers moved around the pattern of the rune on the stone, and he could have sworn that it felt like a capital M. In all this time he had not actually looked, but just moved the stone around in his hand. He then realised that Tommy and Charlie were watching him as he had been deep in his thoughts.

Mr Pilcher spoke again. "I may not be around for a while but I will be back, I'll tell everybody I'm going to see a relative or something, should you need advice you can come and find me in a couple of weeks. You see this is where I belong, these are my hills to keep watch over, this was my 'Inheritance' and you will need to go farther afield to find yours. I shall see you again soon. Remember to trust in your friends."

With that he turned and started to walk off back out across the moor. The boys were all stood absolutely amazed at what was happening. A whole new world had just opened before them. One that they had only read about in books, watched on tv or had heard about in class, but now it was actually real, and they were in the middle of it, part of it, part of history.

There was a thin strip of fog remaining around them, hanging a few feet off the ground, but it would soon be gone. The sun was rising high and was now bright in the clear blue sky above them. There was a peaceful feeling in the air as the boys walked back towards Crich. Charlie had dug out three bars of chocolate from his bag and handed them out which had made Zain extremely happy, rewarded to say the least. The fog must have disorientated them earlier as they were a long way off where they thought that they were going to be, even Charlie had thought that the Shuck Rock was somewhere else on the moor. He looked back in the direction that they had come and true to his memory the Shuck Rock was no longer there, however, it was or as far as he could make out on the ridge in the distance. But that didn't make sense. Could there be two rocks that looked the same but from different angles?

It was a question to be answered at a later date as they did not have the energy to return to investigate further and after all it was the rune stone that had guided them to their destination. The Shuck Rock may have just been a distraction to mislead people if they did not have the rune to guide them.

"What did he mean by 'His inheritance', he doesn't own all of this land up here does he?"

"No, it's part of the farm at the end, well I think it is anyway. He means the rune stones, well it's something to do with that. Did you see how he chose that object out of the bag? I could hear loads of things rattling around. But he. He was letting it come out at random. Do you reckon he can use the runes to read the future?" said Charlie.

"Charlie really! Do you think that a stone can tell you what is going to happen in the future?" said Tommy.

"I don't know any more, Tommy, there's a lot I don't understand at the moment."

Zain had been quiet since Pilcher had left and had been trudging along behind Tommy and Charlie. He now possessed two rune stones and had not yet shown the others what the second had looked like. Did they not care? He checked over his shoulder and then looked all around to make sure that they were alone. "Wait. You haven't asked to see it yet."

Tommy and Charlie had both stopped and turned around to look at Zain. Tommy crouched down and sat on a rock that had fallen off the wall along the side of the path. He gave Charlie a quick nod. "You tell him, Charlie."

"It's yours to look after, Zain, it's never been up to Tommy or me. When you are ready to show us then that's when it will be. Hey, when you do though, there better be a cup of tea and some biscuits, you know what I mean. We're all here together because we need each other, being in control of the stones is your part, what 'we' have to do I don't know, apart from being good looking, eh, Tommy?"

"You said it, mate." Tommy was pushing his chest out and holding his chin upwards. "Emma only goes for the rugged, handsome and adventurous type, hey."

"Don't you dare tell her anything! But seriously, Zain, like Pilcher said, you, no I mean we, need to understand the runes to know what to do next. Thing is you seem to have a bit of a knack with it and we don't."

"C'mon, let's get back to my house." Zain was ready to get indoors and out of the cold.

———————

Charlie finished stirring in the sugar for Tommy and placed the three cups of tea on to the coffee table. Zain had grabbed a few biscuits out of the cupboard and brought them through to share out. He definitely felt like he deserved a treat and that was the best that he could find in the kitchen.

"Hey, Charlie just think if only you had been looking west, towards the village when we were talking to Pilcher on Friday night, well you would never have seen the light and we wouldn't be here now." Tommy had dunked his biscuit for far too long and was now almost slurping it up off the edge of his cup.

Zain had sat in the armchair and had decided that it was only right for them to all see what they had gained. When Pilcher took the brooch from them it had been bitter, but he had in return given them something. He took out the pouch that he now kept the runes in and placed it on the table to his side, opened it and took them out. He selected the new stone and held it out towards his friends.

"I guess this is what we need to work on next, hey?"

It was not quite as they had all expected. It was different in appearance to the first rune stone except the fact that it too, was oval in shape and had a carved marking on it. It was slightly smaller and a different colour. Charlie and Tommy closed in to get a better look. Zain could see that it was as he had felt earlier on the moor. The rune itself looked like a capital letter 'M'. They all knew that it wasn't but that's what it looked like. They now had to find out what it represented and if it worked the same as the first.

"I don't get it, lads, why does it look different?" asked Tommy wiping biscuit from his mouth.

"Good question, Tommy, we need to look in to this. That could take some time though," said Zain.

"Lots of time is what we don't have. I do know one thing though, Zain, we've got some planning to do because next weekend we need to be on it and ready to be wherever it is that we need to be because it looks like we are going to have to venture farther than Crich if we want to know more. If old Pilcher has told us the truth the next full moon is about twenty days away and that takes us into winter. There'll be snow on the hills."

The End

THE CHILDREN
OF THE MOOR
BOOK 2

THE SONS OF WODEN

"Old man and child beware, when the moon is round and full.
For the 'Children of the Moor' will cometh.
They'll seek you out and bind you up,
and turn you all to Woden."

Derbyshire saying, origin unknown.

.